RISE & SHINE

Patrick Allington is a writer and editor. His fiction includes the novel *Figurehead*, which was longlisted for the 2010 Miles Franklin Literary Award, as well as short stories published in *Meanjin*, *Griffith Review*, *The Big Issue*, and elsewhere. His nonfiction and criticism have also appeared widely. Patrick is a former commissioning editor of the University of Adelaide Press. He has taught politics, communications, writing, and editing, most recently at Flinders University. He lives in the Adelaide foothills with his family.

To Zoë, Thomas, Millie, and Laura

RISE
&
SHINE

PATRICK ALLINGTON

SCRIBE

Melbourne • London

Scribe Publications
18–20 Edward St, Brunswick, Victoria 3056, Australia
2 John St, Clerkenwell, London, WC1N 2ES, United Kingdom
3754 Pleasant Ave, Suite 100, Minneapolis, Minnesota 55409, USA

First published by Scribe in Australia and New Zealand 2020
This edition published by Scribe in North America 2021

Typeset in 11.5/17 pt Adobe Caslon Pro by the publishers

Printed and bound in the UK by CPI Group (UK) Ltd,
Croydon CR0 4YY

Scribe Publications is committed to the sustainable use of natural resources and the use of paper products made responsibly from those resources.

9781950354429 (US paperback)
9781925849769 (Australian paperback)
9781925938364 (ebook)

A catalogue record for this book is available from the National Library of Australia.

scribepublications.com
scribepublications.com.au

'The world is so dreadful in many ways.
Do let us be tender with each other.'

— Katherine Mansfield,
letter to Dorothy Brett, 14 August 1918

The end, when everything seemed lost, turned into the beginning. And in the beginning, there was Barton and Walker. No one who survived could really say whether it was a single big catastrophe, or a series of smaller messes, or if it was just the slow grind of excess. Probably it was all of that. Maybe Russia dropped a bomb on San Francisco. Maybe it didn't. Maybe the Nile became poisoned. Maybe it didn't. Maybe the last of the ice caps turned yellow. Maybe they didn't. Maybe Vitamin C turned out to be carcinogenic. Maybe it didn't. Governments of all brands, the UN, the anti-UN, the World Bank, FIFA all spoke loud and long about what needed to happen, but by then no one could tell information from lies.

The details hardly matter now. The earth, pushed past its limits, began to eat its own. Most of the eight billion victims died over a period of a few months. Quickly, slowly: these things are relative. Living another day, and another, depended on who you were and where you were. The survivors tried to eat and drink in the same way that they always had, even as they saw carp floating in rivers, even as dust invaded cities and towns, even as rain pierced skin, even as the tides went wherever they wanted.

Barton and Walker, friends since childhood, dragged themselves around their city — the city that became Rise. They looked for but never found loved ones, joined small bands when it seemed safe to do so, abandoned them at the first hint of violence, skirted fires (except when they needed to try to boil water), avoided dirty lakes where no lakes had previously sat, and took their chances by swallowing what they could scavenge.

Picture them — Walker looking like a boy but for his height, Barton already looking like herself — slinking through the centre of the city, drawn by rumours of a supermarket intact under the rubble. They are filthy. Their clothes are rags. The stress of their situation, the city's situation, the planet's situation, is etched on their faces. They are alive, unlike their parents, their siblings, most of their friends, but they know — they've talked about it, reconciled themselves to it — that they shouldn't be and that they won't be soon.

They find no supermarkets that night. There are none left to find; there is very little of anything to find, other than rumours and innuendo. But they do encounter a small group of people who have surrounded a shirtless man who sits on the ground in the middle of the faded bitumen road. The man wears a see-through bandage that covers one hand and runs all the way to his shoulder.

He shakes his arm, which looks distorted under the plastic bandage.

'I can't feel it,' he says. 'I can't feel my arm.'

Barton crouches in front of him and takes a knife from her pants. 'It's okay,' she says to the man.

'Give her a moment,' Walker says to the crowd, some of whom have slipped their hands into pockets, fingering their own weapons. There is no rule of law now, other than one-to-one negotiation.

Barton makes a careful cut into the bandage at the shoulder end. She puts the knife away, easing the tension, and begins — slowly, slowly — to unravel the plastic. The arm reveals itself, withered by burns, covered in bruises and lumps, and hanging loose as if the bone has turned to rubber. Now that Barton has removed the bandage, it's apparent that the man's wrist is so twisted that his hand faces the wrong way.

Something about this man captivates the crowd. Not just the arm or the way he continues to swing it about, but all of him: his spirit, his hopeless resilience. They stare at him, frankly. He lets them. Walker glances at Barton. Her hand rests on her belly and she has the oddest look of hope — and, almost, contentment — on her face. She meets Walker's gaze. Sees his puzzlement.

'Look again,' she whispers. 'Look harder.'

He looks. He feels. And he begins to understand.

* * *

Cleave was the only person left on earth who looked back, and she did so constantly. Almost absently. No one else in the city-states of Rise or Shine dared indulge the past, except for fleeting glances, a few minutes at a time at most. To dwell on the Old Time, to think about everyone and everything lost, to remember the way the world hovered brazenly on the precipice of disaster for so long before it all unravelled: no one, except for Cleave, could bear it.

It wasn't that Cleave cared less than the rest of them. But she had a job to do and she had no time for emotional turmoil. She often asked herself how anyone from the Old Time could possibly have been surprised by what happened. She didn't think people were stupid, on the whole, but she did think they were malignantly complacent.

As Chief Scientist for what was left of humanity, Cleave's job was to look back, to look forward, to look at the here and now. All at once. Aided by drones, robots, and four walls of autoscreens in the main room of her private compound, she observed and tended to the earth. By donning a headset, she could stay home but roam what used to be Shanghai, days before the fireball, and compare and contrast it with the concrete-studded swamp it had become. She could test the water for toxicity, for salinity, for pathogens. She could scan for signs of plant and animal life. Shanghai, the bottom of the former Pacific Ocean, the polar caps, the Amazon rainforests, a bend in the Volga River, a hamlet in the Hamptons. She could go anywhere, anytime. She saw everything.

Cleave hadn't stood in the same room as another human being for over twenty years. Her private compound was her world. She served the people of Rise and the people of Shine, but she could not share their space. She needed solitude to think. Because of this, she had long ago removed herself from the people she most loved. But she thought about them, her old friends with new names. When she was lonely — it didn't happen often, but it did happen — and she needed to remind herself of the importance of her work, she thought back to the day they had founded the New Time. Walker, Barton: the two of them standing together, already eminent, a little apart from Cleave and the others. Curtin, Holland, Hail, and her. The six of them gathered on a gentle slope in the foothills overlooking a city of rancid air and lingering fires and floods, the place stripped of plants and animals, even rats, the people bereft, sick, starved, bloody, dazed.

'We're going to need an enemy if we're going to make this thing work,' Walker had said that day.

'I'll be the enemy,' Barton had said. She was the bravest of us all, Cleave thought.

They'd been so young then, the six of them. Cleave knew it was plain good luck that they'd found a solution, even if Walker and Barton were a couple of geniuses. Thirty years later, all six of them were still alive. That was a miracle too, though, like everyone, Cleave had tumours to treat and joint pain to endure.

* * *

In the pitch black, a plastic parrot began to whistle 'Singin' in the Rain'. It was a forlorn tune to start another day, less nostalgia and more a warning, a reminder that, in the Old Time, people used to love rain, used to open their mouths to it, used to dance in its muddy puddles, used to store and draw on its bounty. It was a reminder too that birds used to fly about. That they used to exist.

The blackness began to ease, as if the parrot's circling were the day's energy source. On the reconstituted-plastic wall opposite the bed, the image of a tropical garden slowly appeared: glistening deep-green fronds, rustling in a gentle breeze. Impossible. It began to rain, but only on the image on the wall. Gentle but persistent strands of water ran from the ceiling to the floor.

Between them, the plastic parrot and the fake rain woke Walker. That's how it was every morning, now that he wasn't capable of rousing himself at 4.00 am, ready to save the world for another day. He lay face down on the huge, hard bed: he dared not sleep on a mattress he might sink into, unable to get up. His naked body was indistinct beneath a cotton-like plastic sheet. He muttered gibberish, his words up-ended, as the parrot continued to loop the room. Finally, he raised his head groggily, let out a deep sigh — of exasperation and pain, to begin with, and then of resignation — and hauled himself off the bed. When his left foot touched the floor, he winced. When his right foot touched the floor, he cried out. As he stood, crooked, the parrot accelerated and flew straight at the wall above the bed. A small compartment opened for it, then closed, killing the birdsong. The rain eased. The wall of plants became a panoramic window, allowing Walker to survey the city-state of Rise, built on the shell of a city from the Old Time.

He stood dead still, his profile a thin, wasted frame — sunken chest, raw nipples, grandstanding windpipe — staring at his city. His creation. His eyes were lost in their sockets and bloodshot, his cheeks pockmarked, his skin flaky and riddled with sores. Like a cruel joke, his gut was distended and hard. The private Walker was a devastating, inexplicable, pitiable sight.

But as he woke fully, a task he found harder each day, he rallied. His features rearranged themselves into a look that conveyed eminence and calm. Yes, his nakedness told an undeniable, untellable truth. Yes, he was desperately sick. Yes, he was hungrier than he had ever been in his life, hungrier than he thought possible. And yes, he had dry-coughed through yet another night of half-sleep. But too bad. He had responsibilities, the first of which was keeping up appearances. It was no small thing. Step one of the day, he told himself this morning and every morning, was to get himself under control before anyone saw him. His mind as well as his appearance. What other choice did he have? He was Walker: everything depended on him. Well, him and Barton. He never forgot that the survival of the human race was so much her achievement, even if the people of Rise tended to downplay her role and tended, in a friendly but emphatic way, to look down on her city-state of Shine.

Two more deep, searing breaths and his mind was ready. But he couldn't fix his body by himself.

'Enter,' he said, speaking into his wearable, a thin silver-coloured band on his wrist.

A door whirred open and four people scurried into the room. A woman and a man approached Walker first, each of them holding dry cloths. They did not greet him: Walker preferred silence first thing in the morning, because he wasn't yet ready; because this routine was, he felt, a dirty secret; because until these people had done their work, he didn't consider himself to be Walker.

He forced himself to keep his eyes open. Although he didn't enjoy them working up close, putting their hands all over him, it seemed disrespectful to their honest and necessary work not to watch and appreciate it. He lifted his arms perpendicular to his body. The woman wiped the skin of his right side with a cloth, starting at his head and working down. The man started at his left foot, then right foot, left ankle, then right ankle, and worked his way up the legs. The woman and the man cleaned in silence, briefly nodding in solidarity to one another when they met at Walker's midriff. Walker noticed, and it occurred to him for the first time that they might be seeing each other outside of work. What a way to meet a partner, he thought to himself: while anointing a shell of a man.

Once the woman and the man were done, a nurse began dressing the sores and scabs on Walker's body. Walker had a team of health professionals on call, a necessity he found self-indulgent and in contempt of everything he'd fought for in his life. They were led by Curtin, who now hunched close to Walker, attempting to replace the worn-out patch on his chest so that she could check his vital signs. As the Chief Medical Officer, Curtin kept the whole of Rise alive. If at all possible, she kept them healthy and kept them from worrying too much about themselves. She presided over the system that kept in check the tumours the population all had, she watched illness and muscle-pain trends, she monitored grief levels, she examined the causes each time a citizen of Rise died. But these days, she spent more and more of her time with one patient. Walker hated that this was so. He did not want a personal doctor. Curtin had more important things to be doing, so far as he was concerned. Yet Curtin was clear: 'Now is not,' she told him often, 'a good time for you to die.'

She found a piece of Walker's skin that was healthy enough to accept a new patch. But Walker raised a hand to hold her back.

'Not today,' he said. 'Please.'

There was no quaver in Walker's voice when he spoke, Curtin noted, in contrast to his sleep-time voice, which was full of moans and mutterings. Even in his current state of disarray, Walker's waking voice sounded like a choir from the Old Time. He sang the song of reassurance, of 'we'll get through this'. Curtin felt a surge of admiration for her old friend. But she wasn't taken in.

'Sorry,' she said, pushing the patch onto his skin just south of his right nipple. 'Got to be done.'

Curtin stepped back a pace and watched the nurse continue to dress the sores. She doubted that Walker could last much longer: she knew more about the passage of this top-secret illness than anyone else in Rise. She worried that he would die — that she would fail to keep him alive — but she worried just as much that he would live on, his mind a fog, his delirium messing with his legacy. She knew she had to do what she could — just as Walker was always pushing on — and help him in whatever ways she could for as long as she could.

'Must you hover?' Walker asked her.

'I must,' Curtin said.

'Couldn't you leave me in peace for a few minutes, if you've finished poking and prodding?'

'I'll go when I'm ready. A couple of those sores are showing signs of infection.'

Walker sighed, but he was more irritated at himself than at Curtin. He had broken his own rule by speaking during this distasteful ordeal. How could he ask for discipline and forbearance from others, his ever-patient inner circle, if he couldn't manage it himself?

The nurse glanced back at Curtin, a worried look on his face. The two of them crouched down next to Walker's groin, examining a particularly nasty sore, murmuring to each other about infections and pus and dust. Walker, despite his best efforts at serenity, or at least neutrality, began to tap his foot.

'Stand still, please,' Curtin said.

'That's easy for you to say: you're not being *examined*. What are you grinning at?'

'It's good to see you making a fuss,' Curtin said. She murmured and pointed. The nurse shot a dart of white powder into the wound. 'Good. But there too,' she said. 'And there. One more. That'll do.' She stood upright and said to Walker, 'We'll need to do that every three hours for a couple of days.'

'I can't wait,' he said.

She drew nearer. 'It's seeping. And it's sitting close to a tumour.'

The man and woman who had wiped Walker clean now placed a loose white shirt over his head. It had buttons on the front — pure decoration — and a zip that ran from hem to armpit. As the woman eased the zip up — carefully, to avoid a scab that had finally hardened — the shirt inflated with air, filling out Walker's wasted frame, squaring his shoulders, and hiding his bloated stomach.

The man, meanwhile, helped Walker step into a pair of loose trousers, and then swabbed his feet in cloth. Walker stepped into a pair of soft shoes with hard soles. The fact that he managed it by himself gave him confidence that this was going to be a good day.

A final touch: the man took a fresh cloth and rubbed, ever so gently, the sores and scabs on Walker's face, scalp, neck, hands, and wrists. Within a minute, his exposed skin glowed with the appearance of good health.

Walker was finally ready for the day: the well-toned, still-handsome, universally loved ageing saviour, fully dressed, fully lacquered, fully himself. His belly lay in swollen anonymity beneath the shirt. His sores and scabs fought the antiseptic powder in silence. His brain ached but was as sharp as ever.

Walker dismissed the woman, the man, and the nurse one at time by gripping their hands in his, nodding briefly, bowing slightly. Curtin clapped her hands on his puffed-up shoulders, and they leant into each other, foreheads kissing.

'Good luck,' she said.

As Curtin left, Walker's Chief of Staff, Hail, bustled through the same door, giving her hand a squeeze as he passed.

'Mornin', boss,' Hail said. 'Sleep well? Pleasant ablutions?'

Walker stared at him, exasperated by the stupidity of this line of questioning, which was exactly the reaction Hail had been hoping for. In Hail's view — it was just a theory, but a theory he'd trusted for three decades — Walker was at his best when he was mildly irritated. And so Hail made it his business to be a much-needed pain in the arse.

'Hey, I'm just askin'. Just being polite. Friendly. Making conversation,' he said.

'Did I sleep well? For fuck's sake. I haven't slept well for months. As you well know. Last night, I dreamt I was dead. As I might well have been.'

'That's the spirit. Well, we've got a busy day ahead: are you ready to try to eat?'

'Why not? What's another half-hour of my life floating away like dust?'

'Excellent.' Hail spoke into his wristband. 'Okay, people, let's roll: let's give breakfast a whirl.'

The panoramic window opposite the bed became a screen again, showing footage of a group of soldiers in a trench shooting at another group of soldiers in a distant trench.

'Yum,' Hail said. 'Let's eat.'

***

Walker's compound sat in the barren foothills on the eastern edge of Rise. Down the slope, the inner districts ringed the city centre: a few hundred thousand survivors and their offspring. In the outer districts to the west, far from where Walker stood, lived the confused and the edgy and the grief-stained. They weren't outcasts exactly, but they couldn't find a way to embrace the New Time with gusto.

Beyond the fringes was the desert area that still went by its old name of Grand Lake. The desert separated Rise from the city-state of Shine. Rise and Shine: the only two places, so far as the far-flung drones could determine, where human beings still lived. New cities built over old cities, plastic over stone and brick and wood and concrete.

At the same moment that Walker and Hail stood in the bedroom facing an image of war on a wall, the central business district of Rise came to a standstill. The crush of pedestrians heading to work and traffic — midget cars leaning close to plastic roads, the wheels for show — paused as huge autoscreens, made of nothing but the footage itself, appeared out of thin air.

In the main, the citizens of Rise wore happy and expectant faces as they gazed at the autoscreens, even if straightforward exhilaration was impossible. People liked to eat, after all. And a designated mealtime in a public space gave people a chance, a reason, to gaze upwards. Yes, the sky was always out there somewhere, beyond the tallest buildings. But on the whole, people preferred to avoid remembering it was there. The filters did their work, cleaning the air of poisons and bitterness. And at the slightest fear of rain, the domefield covered Rise.

But a citizen called Malee wasn't happy or expectant. Born in the Old Time and now in her mid-forties, she was a data analyst: like the majority of the population, she ultimately worked for Cleave, the reclusive Chief Scientist. Pausing on her way to the office, Malee looked up at the nearest autoscreen, the same as everyone around her. She did her best not to let her disinterest in the war footage show. There had to be another way to do this, she had come to feel, another way to feed the people. Malee didn't know another person in Rise who felt the way she did, although she couldn't believe she was unique. She was uneasy. Dissatisfied. But she was also grateful to be alive. She was grateful to have something to eat. She was grateful that she wasn't muddled, like those poor people living on the western fringes.

***

At the same moment that Malee was gazing up, feeling her isolation, preparing to eat, individual autoscreens appeared in every home in every district in Rise. In House

28, Road 83.2, in the perfectly respectable District 7, a family of four — Geraldina, Flake, and their children, not yet named — sat formally together, heads turned towards an autoscreen at the end of the dining table.

'We give thanks,' Geraldina said.

'We do. We give thanks,' Flake said. He reached out, took Geraldina's hand, and squeezed it. 'Come on, children: give thanks.'

'Thanks,' the girl said.

'Yeah, okay, thanks,' the boy said.

* * *

A battalion, each soldier a household name, was caught in a firefight. For a long moment, the camera held back, as if making sure that the whole population of Rise was paying attention. And they were, even Malee. As she gazed up, she remembered her younger sister, Prija, who hadn't survived the old times. She remembered the purple lump that had grown out of Prija's ear, killing her in a matter of days. Malee often thought of Prija when she ate. The growth had been some sort of cancer, Malee presumed, but she'd never found out for sure. In the chaos, the outsourced authorities had simply taken Prija's body away and burnt it with all the others.

The panoramic view of the battle included the whole cracked, parched field, a tiny patch of the once serene if tourist-infested, the once wet, the once fish-filled, mosquito-breeding Grand Lake. Under a vast cloud of pale red dust, the soldiers danced their desperate dance. They waved guns that discharged bullets designed to wound, not kill. They wrestled with rocket launchers that delivered vibrant, fearful, non-lethal explosions. They yelled and gesticulated. They completed their moves like the experts they were, avoiding the bullets and bombs and manoeuvres of the enemy, a battalion from Shine. This particular battle was going poorly for the soldiers of Rise, which meant that it would go very well for the hungry people of Rise.

Soon enough, the film homed in on a single soldier: Sergeant Sala, a veteran of many campaigns. Sala was pushing thirty, a ripe old age for a foot soldier, or so her friends in the battalion enjoyed telling her. She wore a hard plastic helmet that covered the top and back of her head, including most of her black hair, but which left her face exposed and filthy.

Sala crouched behind an isolated boulder. Perhaps she was waiting for the right moment to retreat. Perhaps she was preparing to launch a daring and futile counterattack. Whatever her intentions, she was trapped.

'Fall back. Fall back now,' yelled Holland, Sala's commander.

A hero to the people of Rise, Holland had stood beside Walker and Barton when they created the New

Time. These days, he went to war miked up. Malee, watching from the central business district, and Geraldina and Flake, watching from home, heard Holland loud and clear. But Sala, the person who most needed to fall back, heard nothing but artillery and an all-too-familiar ringing in her ears. It had reached the point where she could hear the ringing and not much else, even during the long hours between battles, even when she was on leave (not that she liked taking leave). It was an occupational hazard, the army medics had told her, which might, just might, pass in time once she stopped going to war. And if not, she'd need a soundtrack planted in her head.

Her audience knew nothing about the ringing in Sala's ears, but they could see that she was trapped. As she peered beyond the rock, rifle at her shoulder, a bullet thumped into her cheekbone. She grabbed at her face with one hand while aiming her rifle with the other, letting loose a burst of shots — brilliantly close to her target, given the circumstances — as she sprinted to the trench and leapt into it. As she fled, the enemy chose not to shoot her in the back. It wasn't that sort of war.

Sprawled in the trench, her legs twisted sideways beneath her torso, she held her bloody head in her hands. For a moment, it seemed as if she might stay passively where she had fallen, waiting for someone to come and carry her to safety. But Sala roused herself. This was, after all, the moment she had trained for, the exact reason she'd chosen to become a soldier. She stood up and dropped her hands to her sides, ensuring that her audience could see her face. Walking purposefully — not dawdling, not rushing, and with her rifle slung over her bloodied shoulder — she picked her way through the trench.

Soon enough, she found the rest of her battalion. A few of them were nursing minor wounds. Some of them were hacking up dust, and some of them were staring up at the sky, a sure sign of shock. One by one, they saw Sala, saw the blood, saw the skin on her cheek flapping about. Each of them knew that this was Sala's moment. Her friend Kall was the first to break down, and then the rest of them — Duncen, Graice, Benn, Noot, and the others — joined the chorus of wails. Commander Holland himself, clearly deeply moved but far too distinguished to cry in public, held a white cloth to Sala's face.

On autoscreens everywhere, the people of Rise now saw a replay of the shooting of Sergeant Sala. When viewed in extreme slow motion, the bullet entered her face almost tenderly, easing back the skin above her cheek. Frame by frame, that side of her face broke apart. Then the people saw the moment of impact from behind: the jolt of Sala's head, followed by a spray of blood, bone, and cartilage, framing the helmet. Then they saw it from above, the best view for the splatter pattern. And then the screen blurred and the people heard the sound of bullet hitting flesh, followed by the low grunt that Sala deigned to emit.

As the autoscreens slowly turned to black, the chorus of the famous song 'Let's Be Tender' swelled. Once the image had vanished completely, the song faded too. The autoscreens stayed entirely black for a long moment, until a message flashed: 'Thanks for watching. We hope you have enjoyed your meal.' After a moment, a second message flashed: 'Thanks be to Walker. Thanks be to Barton.'

***

Walker felt nothing as he watched 'The Battle of Sergeant Sala', although he certainly, and not for the first time, admired the quality of the young woman's soldiering. It was a fine film. Perhaps, in time, long after his hunger had finished him off, it would be a classic. But it wasn't helping, not in the least, the vast emptiness in his gut. As it finished — 'Thanks be to Walker. Thanks be to Barton' — and as the screen slowly gave way to the panoramic view of Rise, he shook his head, beaten again.

'Well, that was pointless …' He paused, gazing at Hail. 'Oh, hell, what's wrong with you now?'

Hail massaged his temples. 'That was extraordinary, wasn't it? Extraordinary. As good as I've eaten in years.' He gathered himself. 'Well? How was it for you?'

Walker shook his head.

'Nothing?' Hail asked.

'Not a thing.'

'But that poor woman —'

'Soldier.'

'Yes, that poor woman soldier. Her face, that awful moment … didn't it make you want to …'

'I didn't feel a thing, I tell you.'

'It hardly seems possible,' Hail muttered.

'I agree: the footage was brilliant. A bright spot in a ho-hum year. But it did nothing for me.'

* * *

As the autoscreens in the central business district faded, the people recommended walking, riding, driving to wherever they needed to be. The cacophony of noise, the sudden teeming embrace of peak hour, was momentarily harsh, but almost immediately settled into its normal hum. Malee shuffled towards a tall building, a relic of the Old Time, now reclad in green tiles: tasteful or garish, depending on the mood of the sun. She'd eaten, same as everyone else, and she was grateful. Truly she was. But she felt hollow as she took the elevator to the thirty-fourth floor.

A work colleague, Peeter, nodded at her, and the new woman whose name she couldn't remember gave her a friendly wave. She didn't have anything against her co-workers. They worked hard and worked well, and she respected that. And they were all in the business of survival together: she honestly believed that. But she'd tried to chat and be friends with them and go out with them and watch battles with them — Peeter, for a time, had been particularly keen on all that — and she'd just found it too hard. Too false. She was happiest by herself, lost in herself, she'd decided, even if she was lonely.

And these days, she didn't think she trusted herself around other people: her satisfaction with life in Rise had so ebbed that she didn't think she could hide it. She wasn't fearful — Walker was no tyrant, and she gave genuine thanks to him and Barton every day — but she felt an increasing urge to share her worries, vague though they were. To preach. And she found herself thinking about Cleave often. The Chief Scientist hadn't been seen in years. Decades. The human being who knew the most about the earth wouldn't leave her own little bubble, itself inside a city-bubble. Malee sometimes wondered if Cleave and she were kindred spirits. It was probably wishful thinking, she usually concluded.

She typed her password — 'Hungryforsomething01' — and waited for her autoscreen to appear. Her task for the day was to carry on doing what she'd been doing for close to a decade: crunching numbers about weather patterns, both locally and in those parts of the earth where only drones ventured. Specifically, she researched rain: where it fell, what happened to the water once it touched earth. She had no specific idea what happened to her research when she sent it off, no idea what Cleave used it for. She understood the necessity for this: most people who were exposed to the whole story of the state of the earth struggled to carry on. But she still suspected that her main function was to keep herself occupied.

These days, and especially during the last year, it had rained more often, both in the sky over Rise and, according to the satellites and the drones, all over the earth. People hated it when it rained: the domefield enveloped the whole city, the air grew musty, the war out on Grand Lake was postponed. The domefield was a necessary evil that provided essential protection from poisonous water. Except that Malee was starting to think that she knew better. The data she gathered and interpreted hinted at bodies of water that might, just might, be fresh. Clean. Safe. As she settled into her day, receiving data from what used to be called the delta of the Ganges River, an image of Sergeant Sala's exploding face popped into Malee's head. At first, Malee tried to suppress it. But after a moment, she gave in. There was no shame, she decided, in eating well.

* * *

In District 7, Geraldina held her head in her hands, overwhelmed by the tender feelings that washed through her body and mind. Flake patted her back, absently, lost in confusion. The children watched, bemused, as ever, by their hard-feeling parents.

'Can I leave the table?' the girl asked.

'Me too. Can I? Can I?' the boy asked.

'Have you had enough to eat?' Flake asked.

The girl and the boy nodded and bolted from the room, a tangle of arms and legs and giggles. They chased each other to the playroom, where they donned goggles. The floor became a treadmill and they ran through the Old Time, an alien world to them, full of strange lifeforms — animals, they were called — and lurid plants. Their mission was to find the last remaining hippotomus, a six-legged sagging creature with a horn front and back, before it died a natural death, and to sing it a song.

In the dining room, Geraldina still fought to regain her equilibrium, so deeply moved was she by the plight of that soldier. Sala. Some people could eat without limits. But not Geraldina.

'I always love the new footage the best,' she told Flake. 'That poor, poor girl. Did you see her face? So twisted. Do you think there's any chance that she'll heal?'

'I'm still hungry,' Flake said.

'And just like that, she goes from soldier to civilian, as if she's a … like a used cleaning cloth.'

'I said, I'm still hungry.'

'Goodness, are you, love? That's not like you … Do you want to buy the footage? You could watch it again straightaway. It *was* very good.'

'Nah, the new releases are too expensive.'

'We *did* just watch it for free.'

'Let's wait a couple of weeks until the price drops.'

'And we have all those reserves in the bank, and nothing much to spend it on. All I'm saying is, if you're hungry for more of that poor girl, and who could blame you, well, why not buy it? The way her face was there one second and then the next second it was just gone. It gives me the shivers. And the way she carried herself through the pain. My mum would have approved: straight back, straight shoulders, straight neck.'

'I might watch something else. Variety is the spice of life, apparently.'

'My mum used to say that.'

'I know she did.'

'God but I miss her.'

'I know you do.'

'I don't mean just her.'

'I know you don't.'

'I miss all of them.'

They leant together for a moment, Geraldina still as stone, Flake shaking slightly. There was no shame in remembering: Geraldina had been seven when her mother and older sister had disappeared. There was no shame in not remembering, either: Flake's best guess was that he'd been five when things took a turn for the worst. But he couldn't remember his parents, beyond shadows. Siblings? He wasn't sure.

Geraldina roused herself. 'Why don't you watch "The Battle of Bare Hills"? That always fills me up.'

'Ew, not for breakfast. Too heavy. Someone loses an arm in that one, don't they?'

'It was a leg, not an arm. And he didn't actually lose it on the battlefield. But, yes, the surgeon lopped it off just below the knee. What a moment.'

'Ugh, yeah, I remember. Too much for me.'

'What about me giving birth to the boy?'

'Jeez, I'm not that hungry. I've never seen so much blood and guts and pain and suffering.'

'Thank you, love. I was there, you know. On the slab. Living the dream. Smiling for the cameras.'

'You know what I mean.'

'You could watch the highlights of the first eight hours. Just up till the point when things got messy. The miracle of life, and all that. The joy of our very own child.'

'It's a lovely thought, but, nah, not today. Amazing to think, isn't it, that he had so much trouble coming out, when the girl slipped out in seconds?'

'You never actually see the amputation.'

'Eh?'

'In "The Battle of Bare Hills": you never actually see the amputation. While it's happening, you see the soldier's face, the surgeon's face. You hear the whir of the saw. You see that the surgeon drops the leg onto a tray, but you don't actually see the leg. You hear it, oh my God do you hear it. You see the —'

'Somehow that makes it even more unpleasant.'

'But my point is, you don't actually see the actual cut —'

'I'm not feeling all that well, to be honest. I might need to get my tumour checked.'

'Imma from the office claims that it never really happened.'

'What?'

'The amputation in "The Battle of Bare Hills". She says that poor man who got run over by the tank has both his legs to this very day. She says she's seen him, walking around in plain daylight on his own two feet. She says there are people who believe for a fact that none of it's real. That's the way she puts it: "there are people". She's careful not to suggest that she doesn't believe it herself.'

'All that blood and still she doesn't believe what her own eyes tell her. It's no wonder she's so thin.'

'She's got a tumour on her hip. It sticks out. Stretches her clothes something awful, she says.'

'Ew. Why doesn't she just get it removed?'

'In fairness, she exercises a lot. Some days, she does weights *at the same time* that she watches war footage. She swears by the combo.'

'If the war wasn't real, none of us would care. That's basic biology, right? *Right?* If none of us cared, we'd all be dead. I mean, what on earth is she talking about?'

'All right, love. I said I agree with you. No need to

yell at me about it. Take a deep breath. Take another. And another. Good … Look, well, let's just say Imma's got a lot of funny ideas. I like her. She's the life of the party … not that I can remember the last time *we* went to a party.'

'That one we watched today: what was it called again?'

'"The Battle of Sergeant Sala". Evocative title, don't you think? Good of them to name it after that poor, poor girl. It's only right.'

'In that one, you can smell the blood. That's my point. You can literally smell it. There's no way they can fake that.'

'Can we watch "The Battle of Bare Hills" for dinner? Skip the live feed?'

'Well … it's not my absolute favourite.'

'I know, love. But the children love eating vintage.'

'What about I watch the live feed, and then we all watch "Bare Hills" as a family?'

'Perfect,' Geraldina said. 'Now, I'd better get ready for work.'

She patted Flake on the shoulder as she left the dining room. He stayed where he was, waiting to make sure she wasn't coming back, and then put his wearable close to his mouth.

'Buy "The Battle of Sergeant Sala",' he whispered. 'And play it again. Private viewing. On mute.'

The image of Sergeant Sala appeared just past the tip of Flake's nose. Flake's eyes widened. The safety catch on his mouth snapped and his tongue hung free for a moment before he pulled himself back into line.

'Go closer,' he murmured urgently. 'Come on, closer. Closer. Closer, dammit.'

The image became an extreme close-up of Sala's face, eventually focusing on a single pore. But the pixels merged; the close-up wouldn't quite focus.

'Where are you, dear?' Geraldina called.

'Off. Turn *off*,' Flake whispered fiercely.

The image disappeared just as Geraldina entered the dining room.

'There you are. I'm off to work. The kids are in the playroom. Take it easy today, won't you? You've been working too hard. You need some rest.'

Flake nodded, fighting to control his breathing. Geraldina left with a wave.

'Wrong. Very, very wrong,' Flake muttered to himself. Whatever disrespect Geraldina's friend Imma was showing towards the war — towards Walker, towards the feat of survival — Flake knew that his own transgression was far worse. What an awful way to treat a hero. He had no idea what was wrong with him. Perhaps, he hoped, it was just a tumour in his head, leaning on the wrong spot of his brain.

'Play it again,' he whispered to his wearable.

* * *

'Is she here yet?' Walker asked Hail. A few days had passed since the premiere of 'The Battle of Sergeant Sala'. Long enough for the people of Rise to feast. Long enough for the critics to rave. And long enough for Sala to be summonsed from the front line, where for weeks she'd been recuperating from her injuries and then idling while waiting for the premiere of the footage. At last, she'd had the call: a personal meeting with Walker.

'Yeah, she's already in the waiting room,' Hail said. 'We were due to start fifteen minutes ago.'

'Okay, let's do it.'

'Let her down gently, won't you?'

'Don't I always?'

'Holland says she's not happy about it. Not happy at all.'

They left Walker's private quarters and made their way along a long corridor until they came to the words 'Reception Room' painted onto the floor. They stood on the sign, which descended into a room. They stepped off and the sign rose again to the ceiling. Walker positioned himself between two Rise flags.

Hail opened a door. 'Walker will see you now,' he said.

'How many times do I have to remind you?' Walker whispered. 'It's "Walker will meet with you now": "meet with you", "meet with you", "meet with you".'

Sergeant Sala entered. She marched across the room, stiff-armed, and stood to attention in front of Walker. She met and held his gaze, feeling nervous in his presence and yet sure of herself. She wasn't happy, but she was ready.

'Thank you for coming, Sergeant Sala,' Walker said. 'It can't have been easy, these last weeks. The wound. The recovery. Waiting for the footage to debut. It can't be easy still, adjusting to a new life.'

'Thank you for inviting me, SIR. But I wasn't aware that I had much choice but to be here,' Sala said.

'Easy there, soldier,' Hail said.

'Fair enough,' Walker said. 'Congratulations, then, on understanding the reality of your situation. I wanted to thank you personally for your sacrifice. The citizens of Rise owe you so much. I, personally … Is something the matter, Sergeant Sala?'

'I'm sorry, sir, but can I ask you, what's with the flags?'

In truth, Walker wasn't a fan of flags. He was old enough to remember the way bigots wielded them like semi-automatics in the last years of the Old Time. And yet, in the earliest days of Rise, something had compelled him to use them for formal occasions. Perhaps, he had to admit, his motives were base: a little whipping up of mild parochialism was a distasteful necessity. But he liked to think that the flag of Rise, featuring a stylised cityscape nestled within its domefield, gentle red rain falling, meant nothing more than 'it is good that we still exist'.

'You don't like them?' he asked Sala.

'Frankly, they offend me,' Sala said.

'Now, look here —' Hail started, but Walker held up his hand.

'Excellent,' he murmured, mostly to himself. Without turning, he pushed the poles over, leaving the flags prostrate.

'Sergeant Sala: I, personally, owe you so much,' Walker continued, ignoring the shock on Hail's face. 'On Commander Holland's recommendation, I have read your file several times over the years. I've written the odd comment in it myself. I've watched many hours of unedited footage of you. In short, I've followed your progress closely.'

'Makes you sound like a bit of a pervert, sir.' Sala peered hard at him. Up close, she thought, he was shiny. Suspiciously so: was he wearing a mask?

'Sergeant Sala, stand to attention,' Hail said. 'You really are too much.'

'It's fine: at ease, at ease,' Walker said. He smiled a wide smile that hurt his face. 'I didn't expect you to last this long, given the spirited way you fight.'

'Sorry to disappoint you, SIR.'

'You misunderstand me. On purpose, I can see.'

'I'm not just a pretty face, eh?'

Walker allowed himself another smile, but he could feel the dizziness start to impose itself. He fought for balance, as best he could.

'You could always simply accept my compliment,' he

said, 'which is heartfelt and richly deserved.'

'Is that an order, SIR? That I accept your compliment?'

Mostly, Sala wanted to make Hail fret, since he seemed so prone to it. But there was no unsettling Walker, she could see. He was entirely unfussed by her poking and prodding. In fact, he seemed to be enjoying it. And yet something was wrong with him. She could sense it.

'It's not an order,' Walker said. 'Merely a request that you accept the truth: you have been an unusually fine and effective and committed soldier. Not just during your final glorious act, but throughout your career. You have been a magnificent servant of the people of Rise — and of Shine, for that matter. And you have my word that you will get all the personal and professional support you need, now and into the future. You are a hero to the people. Your sacrifice will help feed us for years. I hope that you will find a way to feel proud every mealtime, and that you allow yourself to take pleasure in your conduct.'

'Don't misunderstand me, sir: it's the great honour of my life to serve the people. And it's really quite nice to meet you.'

'Even if you didn't have a choice, eh?'

'I had a choice to serve or not. I had a choice how to serve. But now, in my moment of glory — that's what you just called it, right? — I have no choices. Except to speak my mind.'

Walker stepped forward so that he was very close

to Sala's face, and examined it in forensic detail. She inhaled and exhaled through her nose because she didn't want to breathe on him. But her damaged, half-closed nostril hissed, and the scar tissue throbbed. And while he inspected her, she saw right through his face powder to the wounds beneath. *Shit*, she thought.

'You understand what must happen now?' Walker said.

'I do, sir, but … Yes, I understand. But I want to ask: is there any way, any way at all, that I could stay in my battalion? I love the trenches. I am at peace fighting. I know the rules, but I've thought about this a lot, and I'm certain that I could —'

'Sergeant Sala, I'll say it again: come to attention,' Hail said.

'Ease up there. It's been a big month,' Walker said to Hail. But to Sala he said, 'What you ask is impossible, and you know it. Haven't you looked in the mirror lately? Your legacy will endure, but your work in the trenches is at an end. You're immortal, but you're done. Okay,' he said to Hail, 'let's do this.'

Walker and Hail stood erect and formal, and Sergeant Sala, after considering her options — she had none — followed their lead. Hail read from a document that appeared on a personal autoscreen before his eyes:

'Sergeant Sala, you are hereby honourably discharged from the 4th Armoured Battalion after seven years, eight months, and twenty-five days of service, including six years, nine months, and three days of active combat service. You are released on full pay for thirty years, and four-fifths pay thereafter, index-linked, with free medical treatment, including for all existing and new tumours, until you die. You are released from your obligations with the people of Rise's grateful thanks.'

'And with my personal best wishes for whatever civilian life holds in store for you,' Walker added. 'Is there anything further you wish to say?'

'Please understand me: I don't care about my face. Really, I don't. But I will mourn my lost calling for the rest of my life.'

'I understand. But you've done all you can do.'

'This way, please,' Hail said, taking Sala's elbow. She glanced over her shoulder as she left. She and Walker shared a nod, almost of equals. These days, Walker rarely met another human being who didn't bow and scrape. He would have jumped and cheered, if only he'd had the energy.

Hail returned, patting his tummy contentedly. 'Well?' he asked. 'Did you feel anything then? Seeing her up close must have done it for you.'

Walker shook his head. 'No, nothing,' he said. But he continued to ponder ex-Sergeant Sala. He knew the best of the best. He could sniff them out. Sala was too skilled, too self-possessed, too smart, too brave to disappear into retirement, aged twenty-something.

Hail, meantime, had more pressing matters on his mind. It was his job — increasingly, he thought, it seemed to be his only job — to try to get Walker to eat something. Anything.

'We need to move on to Plan B. I repeat: commence Plan B,' Hail said into his wearable. 'You won't be able to resist this, boss. Not a chance in the world.'

'Oh, the world,' Walker murmured. 'Remember the world?'

The doors opened to admit a grinning, slobbering dog. It staggered into the room, led by a handler, shackled by a plastic rope and noose. Mid-sized, with random sweeps of brown, black, and white hair, the creature moved on four legs of different shapes and lengths. In place of a tail, it had a wagging fifth leg, which may or may not have doubled as a penis. It struggled to walk, stumbling constantly on its gnarled nails. The handler handed the lead to Hail and left the room.

'First dog I've seen in …' Walker said.

'Thirty-four years, give or take,' Hail said, doing the maths for him. 'Say hello to Fred.'

'Is it real? Is it safe? Where the hell did you get it?'

'I picked it up out beyond the badlands. I —'

'What were you doing out there? I've asked you — I've pleaded with you, for Chrissakes I've ordered you — to stay away from the outlying sectors.'

'What's the problem? Cleave's always sending people

out there these days. Think of it as the outer suburbs of Rise.'

'Cleave doesn't give those people a thought. It wouldn't occur to her. Curtin makes sure they're safe.'

'But they go. That's the point. They go.'

'They're highly trained. Scientists in suits, with oxygen tanks, taking precautions before, during, and after. They submit to full-body cleans. They're willing to put up with extra tumours. They aren't forever walking into walls.'

'Oh, be fair: I only did that once. Weeks ago. And I'd been watching battle-scene edits for ten hours straight. Anyway, what makes you think I found Fred myself?'

'Because you're the worst micromanager I've ever met.'

'Surely you mean the best?'

'Surely you jest?'

'Well, look, I only go out there because I care about you. I worry about you. And I can't exactly tell these experts of yours what I'm looking for and why, now can I? Besides, the purple sunsets out there are incredible. You should come out with me for a look sometime. Really.'

'And if you go and grow a second head, or an arm spontaneously appears out of your arse, or a tumour twice your body weight erupts in your armpit, how the hell will I explain that to the media? There's no escaping the rain out there. Seriously: I hope you are taking proper precautions. Don't go getting complacent about survival.'

In truth, Walker knew that Hail didn't only go to

the badlands to try to scavenge food for him. He knew that Hail had always felt trapped by the confines of Rise, and especially by being stuck day after day in Walker Compound. Hail missed the great expanse of the world, now off limits, as if it weren't there at all. In the Old Time, Hail would have chucked a backpack in the back of a brick of a car and followed his nose out beyond mountain ranges and deserts.

Walker peered at the dog. 'Have you had that thing checked for diseases? What's its radiation count?'

'Fully approved by Cleave and by the good doc. Let's just say we can be confident that Fred is a hell of a lot healthier than you.'

'So it might last the week, then?'

'Okay, watch this: sit, Fred. Good boy. C'mon, sit. Sit, boy. Sit, Fred. You can do it, Fred. Go on, Fred.'

The dog did its best to sit, but it couldn't quite work out how to make its limbs behave. It seemed as if its every breath were designed to make it collapse in on itself. Hail grinned on. Walker watched reluctantly, dismayed and yet unmoved. Not for the first time that week, he asked himself if he were still human. The dog tried again, managing a crouch.

'Jeez, how long have you had it?' Walker asked. 'How did you train it?'

'We have our methods. Don't think about it. Enjoy the show.'

With a whimper, the dog leapt into the air, performed a midair flip, and landed with a heavy thump on its side. It lay on the floor, panting, wagging its tail that was actually a leg. Hail stared intently at Walker, who ran his tongue around his teeth.

'Anything?' Hail said.

'Something. Not much. But something …'

'Do you need it to do it again? Take two, Fred. Up, Fred, up.'

'No no no. That'll get me through the day. Maybe. Probably. Let's get on with things. But help the dog up first. It's unbearable.'

'Are you kidding?' Hail said. 'No way I'm touching that thing.'

***

Grainy — thirty-one years old, a child of the chaotic early years of the New Time — still wasn't feeling well. It had been like this for weeks. At first, he hadn't thought much of it. Yes, both of his parents had died at about his age. But they'd had that wasting disease that had finished off some of the Old Time people in the early days of Rise. Once you had it, there was no getting rid of it: regrettable but inevitable, the official line went. And fair enough, Grainy thought. The New Time doctors weren't responsible for Old Time failings. It was just as well he thought that way, because right now he was sitting in a doctor's waiting room, pretending not to be nervous.

Grainy had got himself body-scanned in his twenties, just to be sure he wasn't carrying the wasting disease. The robot had given him the all clear. And that's exactly what nagged at him. Why wouldn't the unwellness pass? He was too young to be moving into the second stage, let alone the final stage, of life. His genes were sound. His tumour rubbed the back of his knee, but it was small and lax. There was no good reason for him to feel the way he felt.

Perhaps, he thought, it was just that the air quality had been going through a bad patch, what with the increase in rain, what with the announcement that the authorities would be upgrading the domefield, what with the persistent high winds blowing in from the western badlands. The people who Grainy shared his life with all had their problems. His ex-partner Mace often had a severely swollen left ankle. He knew because he lived a floor above her: he often went down and shared an autoscreen at dinnertime with Mace and their child, who they really needed to name, given that she was nearly nine years old. Some days, he massaged Mace's ankle while they ate, the little girl putting a hand on each of them.

Grainy's friends — some from his work at the Institute of Peace Studies, some acquired during his years living in the Walker Home for Children of Parents of the Old Time Who Did Not Survive — were always complaining about transient aches or pain or stiffness. Periodic discomfort — low-level, a mere irritant — was normal. It was part of the business of having survived, of living in the New Time. Every doctor was a physio. Every partner was a masseuse. Every mattress vibrated hot or cold on request.

So Grainy hadn't been worried, initially, that he felt off. But whatever ailed him did not come and go. Nor did it obviously announce itself. And the pain wasn't predictable. It didn't find a weak spot, like his tumour had done. Once the nagging feeling that he should be worried took hold, he'd tried to record his medical history. The problem had started, hadn't it, with a dull ache in his gut, then his fingertips, all ten of them, mild but undeniable, then his gut again, then his right shoulder. But after that, the order became hazy. Now the ache had spread throughout his body. He felt wrong everywhere. And his skin was beginning to rebel. He'd never had sores, not even after that time, fifteen years ago, maybe more, that the domefield and the backup domefield had both malfunctioned and Rise had been sprinkled with a couple of minutes of light rain.

Most of all, whatever the nature of the illness, Grainy was desperately tired. He wasn't spending enough time with the child, that light-filled girl who dreamed of joining the war. He was neglecting his friends. He was demurring when Mace asked him to rub her ankle, and he liked rubbing her ankle. He wasn't pulling his weight at work. He knew it, and he felt awful. Peace was important. Peace was everything. Peace took time and effort, day in, day out, like breathing.

Finally, when he realised his gut was turning hard, the worry wore him down. He went to the doctor for the first time since he'd mysteriously snapped his Achilles tendon, before his twentieth birthday. He still had no idea how he'd done his Achilles. It hadn't been fussed over at the time: old Doc Bille, a genius neurosurgeon in the Old Time whose hands, in the New Time, shook, just slightly but more than enough, had watched and nodded as a couple of trainee nurses ripped the old tendon out and slipped a new one in. Grainy was home before dark, and pain-free in thirty-six hours. Eventually, old Doc Bille had let his tumours kill him. Or so Grainy had heard.

Today, though, a new doctor, Dr Gee, ushered him into her room and gazed at him with a wounded look as he described his symptoms.

'Is it serious?' Grainy asked. 'It is, isn't it?'

'Remove your clothes, please,' Dr Gee said. She was all business. Under the circumstances, it was the only way.

'What, all of them?'

'All of them.'

'Even my —'

'All of them.'

'Isn't it customary to have a third person in the room,

for such an … an extensive intrusive examination? I mean, we hardly know each other, and I'm a citizen and you're a medical officer, and, and, and —'

'Yes, quite right: Section 9.1.1.1 of the Medical Regulations of Rise. But, sorry, not this time.' Don't push me, she thought. Don't ask questions. Don't doubt me. Let's just get through this, best we can.

'May I ask why?'

'I'm sorry, truly I am, but that's classified information.'

'Classified? But it's my body.'

'All I can do is refer you to Section 12.4.29, amendment 4.'

Section 12.4.29 flashed onto an autoscreen. Grainy started reading: 'Exceptions to Section 9.1.1.1 can be made when a medical officer is instructed by unnamed authorities (see Section 13.84.2.77) that Section 44.1 can be invoked.' On and on it went, exactly the sort of gibberish that the New Time, taking Walker and Barton's lead, had abandoned.

'That bad?' Grainy said.

Dr Gee shrugged. 'Please remove your clothes. Please just do it.'

As Grainy attempted to strip, he grew breathless. The zip on his shirt half-undone, he dropped his arms to his side.

'I'm sorry,' he said. 'I'm doing my best. I really am. I just need a moment. This is the problem, the exact problem, or part of it: I start things, but I don't quite have the energy to finish them.'

'Let me help,' Dr Gee said. She already knew how this examination was going to end, and she was keen to get it over and done with — for her sake and for that of this nice young man. She pulled the zip, exposing Grainy's torso, and pulled the shirt free. His slightly distended belly drew her hand. She shone a light camera on his chest. After a moment, an image, magnified 900 times, materialised before her. Don't ask him any personal questions, she told herself. Just don't.

'Hmmmm,' she said, putting on a show for no good reason. She could see that he knew he was in deep trouble.

She pulled the zip of Grainy's trousers and they fell to his ankles, revealing thin legs, bulging kneecaps, and a lovely round discolouration on his hip that would soon enough turn red and raw. She tugged on his underpants. They dropped without resistance.

'Well? What do you think?' Grainy asked.

'One moment, please.' She gave his stomach one last conspiratorial prod and then turned her back on him. 'I've got a Code 427,' she whispered into her wearable. Goddammit, yet another one, she thought to herself. Six in a week.

Barely fifteen minutes later, two orderlies dressed in sleek black overalls, masks covering their faces, strapped Grainy to a gurney. They placed an especially tight strap across his middle, pushing his swollen belly into his body cavity. Gently, they slipped a cloth mask over his head.

'I'm so sorry about this, truly I am,' one of the masked men said, as he adjusted the mask so that its two holes aligned with Grainy's nostrils. 'A necessary precaution, but I do apologise.'

'I feel bad,' the other man added, 'but you can't talk — please, not a word — until we tell you that you can.'

'But where are you taking me?' Grainy asked.

'I'm most dreadfully sorry but, as I just said, not a word now.'

They carried him out of Dr Gee's surgery via a rear door, loaded him into a windowless van, and drove away. Once they were moving, they lifted the cloth off his face.

'Sorry about that. Truly. A regrettable but necessary precaution.'

'But where are you taking me?' Grainy asked. 'What's going to happen to me?'

'Best-case scenario: you'll be a picture of good health in no time at all.'

'But why won't you actually answer my question? Where are we going? Please tell me what's happening. Have I done something wrong? Committed some crime? Oh, please tell me.'

'No, no, you've done nothing wrong. Not in the least. We're helping you,' one of them said.

'It is what it is,' the other one said, absently patting

Grainy's head. 'Best to make the most of it. Think of it as downtime.'

'But where are you taking me?'

'We're going where we have to go. It's not a long trip. Sit back. Close your eyes. Enjoy the smooth road.'

'You might find it helps to imagine something pleasant. A favourite battle scene, perhaps.'

'Can you at least take these straps off me now?'

'No no no: they're part of the healing process, believe it or not.'

'Is that a gun in your belt?'

'A gun? I'd be very surprised if it was a gun.'

After a longer time than the hooded men had promised Grainy, the van arrived at an imposing gated building from the Old Time. Its old sign was faded but intact: 'National Concert Hall'. The hall was fashioned from great chunks of sandstone, patched up here and there with clear plastic bricks. It was classic Rise architecture: the best of the old combined with the best of the new. The bright colours of the tall, enclosing fence suggested the barrier was a recent addition.

The van pulled up close to the building, and the two men carried Grainy inside. There was no need to cover his face, no need for secrets. He was at his destination and he wasn't going anywhere. He lay silent as they carried him through the labyrinth, trying to keep track of the route: up, down, left, right, up again, down again, right,

right, right. He'd forgotten it all by the time they banged through a set of ornate Old Time doors — actual wood, but now covered in thick clear plastic, squeaky on the hinges — and tacked down a slope until they found a free bed. Only then did they undo the straps and slide him onto a cool, dry mattress.

'Good luck, friend,' one of them said cheerfully, as he clipped Grainy's ankle to the bed. 'That's just so you don't fall off.' And then they were gone.

Grainy lifted his head. He was in a vast room filled with beds and people. The floor angled like a grand curved staircase: there was a row for beds and equipment, then a row for walking, then a row for beds and equipment, then a row for walking, all the way from top to bottom. Dim lights studded the ceiling and the floor, leaving the space inbetween uncluttered, open, regal. Gloomy.

Most of the patients lay in their beds, but here and there one of them was propped up on elbows or sitting up, legs dangling off the side of their bed. A handful of patients — Grainy counted four of them before the gloom in the space defeated him — were wandering back and forth, back and forth, near their beds. Everyone that Grainy could properly see, anyone not camouflaged under a sheet, was terribly thin and wore a big, hard belly. Each of them, even the four or so who were walking, had a battle scene playing in front of their face. But there was no audio. The room was entirely silent, other than the shuffling of feet and bedsheets and the occasional whispered conversation between patients and nurses or doctors.

An autoscreen appeared in front of Grainy's nose. He'd lost track of time, but he doubted it was dinnertime. Still, he was happy enough to watch as Sergeant Sala lost half her face, because why not, because he was so very hungry, because they obviously weren't fussed about anyone overeating.

Beyond the screen, he saw a nurse walking towards him.

'Welcome,' she murmured. 'We're here to help. We'll do everything to fix you that we can.'

'But where am I?'

'Shhhhh,' she said, 'or you'll miss the good bit.' She slid an earpiece into his ear canal just in time for him to hear the bullet thud into Sala's face and for the sergeant to grunt in her 'oh well, it had to happen sometime' way. 'Don't worry,' the nurse said. 'It's on a loop.'

'But why am I here?'

'Oh, they should have told you that before they brought you here. I'll have a word with them, make sure it doesn't happen again,' she said. And with that, she turned and walked away.

'Can I contact my daughter?' Grainy called after her.

'She knows you're safe,' the nurse said, without stopping or turning. 'That's good enough for now, I think you'll agree.'

***

Walker and Hail walked slowly through the lower level of Walker Compound, a series of rooms and buildings, all connected by corridors, tunnels, paved walkways. They received an occasional nod or 'Hello, boss'. One young woman pulled Hail up to get his signature for a fleet of drones to move into a new sector of the former Pacific Ocean.

'Goddamned micromanaging. If Cleave wants a drone, she gets a drone,' Walker muttered.

'It's not about second-guessing anyone. Especially Cleave. It's about balancing resources. It's about keeping track. It's about understanding the big picture. It's about having some idea what she's doing because she'll sure as hell never get around to telling us herself.'

'That's just the way she works, thinking only about the work.'

The young woman looked embarrassed: she didn't really need to witness the great Walker and the near-great Hail bickering. Hail signed with a flourish, and released her to the corridor.

'I don't want to do an interview today,' Walker said.

'You don't want to do an interview any day,' Hail said. He tried to take Walker's elbow, but Walker parried him away. 'I wonder if we should touch up your face before they film you.'

'Didn't I do one last week?'

'It's been nearly three months. It's got to be done. A chance for the masses to hear some words of comfort and grace from the great man ahead of the peace talks —'

'Peace talks blah blah blah. Isn't that why we decided to have a president: to give a running commentary on life, the universe, and the peace talks?'

'Up to a point. But the people do love to hear from you. They need it. As you well know.'

They passed the corridor that led to Cleave's private compound. Walker always felt distressed when he passed it. She'd locked herself in over twenty years ago, built her own micro-world of a few rooms plus a private courtyard. She and Walker spoke when necessary: sometimes three times in a week, sometimes once or twice a month. They had an open line of communication — Cleave could be chatty, when in the mood, at least briefly — and Walker had learnt to make it clear when he needed her urgently, even if she wasn't in the mood. He didn't quite understand why she'd cut herself off. He hoped it was because her brilliance needed solitude. He suspected it was because she couldn't bring herself to be around the rest of humanity when she knew how tenuous life now was. He worried that she was lost in grief, unable to move on from the Old Time when her life's work was to understand what the Old Timers had done to the earth. He had never, or at least not after the first couple of years, tried to talk her out. He liked to think that he respected her decision. Her need for isolation. But that wasn't it. Without her work, they never would have made it, even though she never thought about the practicalities, never understood Walker's priorities, never really connected her work on the world to the health of Rise and Shine. So if this was how she worked, Walker had decided long ago, then so be it.

'It's not a live interview, is it?' Walker asked Hail.

'Of course not. Ajok will edit it herself and submit it back to me for approval. But she's very good. She knows what we need her to do.'

'You should get her to edit some battle scenes. Shake things up a bit.'

'I've been asking her to do that for years. She always says she'll think about it. You could always order her to do it.'

'Don't be unpleasant.'

'Once she's done with you, around 10.45, there's time for Curtin to check you over, if need be. And for you to have a quick nap.'

'I told you, no more naps. I can't be seen to be sleeping all the time. The staff will notice. There are already rumours.'

'After your nap —'

'No nap.'

'Curtin has explained the need for naps to you. You've agreed to naps. We've factored naps into your schedule.'

'Well, I un-agree.'

'Don't be petulant: Curtin says it isn't good for your heart.'

'My heart.'

'Look, we'll stop calling them naps if you think that'll help. All you need do is close your eyes for fifteen minutes. Twenty, tops. Only you'll know if you actually sleep.'

'Curtin will know, with those smart patches stuck all over me.'

'Think of it as an investment in the rest of the day.'

'And you can fuck off with that Old Time management speak. That's how we got into this mess.'

'To be frank, naps are keeping you alive.'

'I thought that dog was keeping me alive.'

'After your nap with a new name — let's call it a "power pause" — we need to go out to Grand Lake. I'm sorry, boss, but I have news: there was another death overnight. Another soldier.'

'What? You're only telling me this now? Why didn't you tell me when it happened?'

'It happened late last night. I didn't want to disturb you.'

'That's not your decision to make.'

'First things first: I wanted you to get some sleep, and after you'd done that — Did you sleep? Did you? Yes, you did — I wanted to try to get you fed. Did I get you fed? Did I? You've had that dog four days in a row, so, yes, I did.'

'You want me to sleep, you want me to talk to Ajok, you want this, you want that, you want to withhold essential information from me.'

'It worked too. If I'd told you about the death at ten to one, which is when I heard about it, there's no way you'd have enough energy to be grumpy at me now.'

'I have to know events in real time: boom boom boom. That's the way I work. Always has been, and must be still.' Walker paused, leant against the wall for a moment, remembered he was in the corridor, and spoke more quietly: 'How'd it happen?'

'Natural causes, apparently.'

'Apparently?'

'This fella decided to do 200 push-ups. One-handed, mind you. I mean, what a grandstander. He probably deserved what he got.'

'And what did he get, exactly?'

'He got to 201, wiped himself down with a towel, and collapsed. Dead before he hit the ground, according to the eyewitnesses. And before you ask, no one filmed it. Pity: could have been something decent to try and feed you with.'

'Don't be crass. That's five in a month.'

'A month and a bit.'

'Curtin needs to autopsy the body to within an inch of its life.'

Hail's wearable buzzed.

'Yes?' he said. 'Is it important? I'm right in the middle of … Ah … Right, okay, never mind … No, thanks for telling me. No, that's fine, you did the right thing … You'd better cut it open, I suppose. Take a look. And let Cleave know you're doing it. She may want the footage or have some instructions … No, I won't ask her. Ask her yourself … You send her a message and you wait. That's what I have to do … Tell her it's urgent and keep the body cold … Right. After the autopsy, just get rid of it. Unless Cleave tells you different … No, just dry burn it. Make sure there's nothing left. Not a hair … Okay, bye.'

'What's happened?' Walker asked.

'Oh, nothing you need worry about.'

'I need to know everything.'

'Okay, okay: the dog died.'

'Of course it did. Some sort of change-of-environment illness, presumably? Not enough radiation in the air here, something like that?'

'Vale Fred,' Hail murmured. And just for a moment, although longer than he knew was wise, he allowed himself to remember his childhood puppy, Missy, who licked and widdled and dug the garden for four and a half glorious months before she slipped through two fence pickets and headbutted a Mazda hatchback.

They stepped into the doorway of the recording room. A nurse, plainly dressed, stood guard.

'For Chrissakes,' Walker said.

'Better safe than sorry,' Hail said cheerfully.

The door slid open, and Hail gave Ajok and the camera crew a friendly wave.

'Just give us a minute, will you?' Hail said.

'Busy saving the world again, eh?' Ajok said, flashing the full-mouthed smile that, as one of Hail's premier interviewers, she had obliged herself to master.

'I want to see the autopsy results for that dog myself,' Walker said to Hail. 'And don't forget to let Curtin know about the autopsy. She loves looking inside dead stuff.'

'Just so long as she keeps the whole thing quiet. We don't want any of those *Medical Journal of Rise* articles she's so fond of dropping on us unannounced. I really wish you'd speak to her about that.'

'She lives and breathes free speech. And for checking my pulse.'

'Sir, I'm sorry to interrupt,' the nurse said, 'but I'm here to check your pulse. And a few other things.'

'Find Curtin,' Hail said into his wearable. He paused for a moment, and then spoke again: 'It's me. Yeah, good morning. We've got a bit of a, um, wildlife situation here ... Oh, you heard ... Well, it was good while it lasted ... Walker thought you might want to watch the autopsy ... Yeah, he's doing fine, all things considered. He's fired up. Your nurse is giving him a look now. But come and see him when we get back from Grand Lake ... You sure? It's not every day you get to see inside a dog ... Yes, all right.

We're leaving soon.' He looked up at Walker. 'Curtin says she's coming with us to Grand Lake. She says if she doesn't come, you're not going either.'

Walker shrugged, and then winced. 'Have you told Willy we're coming?' he asked.

'I wish you wouldn't call him that.'

'It's his name.'

'It used to be his name. It's not helpful, in the current environment, given everything, given the state of your —'

'Stomach.'

'Health and wellbeing.'

'Are we done?' Walker asked the nurse.

'All done.'

Walker stood before the door, which whirred open. 'Right, Ajok,' Walker said. 'It's nothing personal, but let's get this thing over with nice and quick, can we?'

'Most certainly, sir. I just need a few words of comfort and inspiration for your adoring fans.'

'If they really adored me, they'd respect that I am a man of few public words. But sure. I can do that.' To Hail, he murmured, 'So, is Willy expecting us or not?'

'*Commander Holland* has not been officially informed of our intentions. But I doubt he'll be too surprised if we show up.'

'No, tell him. Tell him now. I want him to stew … What was his name?'

'Who?'

'The dead soldier. What was the dead soldier's name?'

'Please, boss,' Hail said, nodding towards Ajok.

'I'm sorry, Ajok,' Walker said. 'I know we haven't even started, but could I trouble you and your team to leave the room for a moment.'

'Of course, sir. No problem.'

'None of that equipment is turned on, is it?' Hail said.

'Certainly not,' Ajok said. She flashed her smile — it was the mandatory full stop to every sentence she uttered, and she felt it, like a prick, every single time. This smile strained, and she could see that Hail knew that he had offended her.

Ajok ushered the film crew ahead of her, backed out of the room, and paced the corridor. She was fiercely loyal to Walker — like everyone born in the New Time, she owed her very birth to him — but she could take or leave Hail. She didn't think he was nasty or even conniving. She just found him a little too big for his boots. And these days, she'd noticed, Hail was always hovering around Walker. It was odd. And vaguely troubling. Why, for example, did he need to be here for this interview? Ajok wondered if she could slip in a question about it on camera: something along the lines of 'There are those who say you are becoming too dependent on too few advisers?' But, no, there was no way of doing it tactfully. Anyway, she knew the boundaries. Believed in them too. Yet she worried that Hail was building a wall, plastic brick by plastic brick, between Walker and the people.

'What is the dead soldier's name?' Walker asked Hail again, once they were alone.

'I don't, um … someoneorother. Smiffee, maybe. Not sure.'

'I know he's not a diseased dog from the badlands, but, all the same, if you could give him a moment's care and attention, I'd appreciate it. Find out his name, eh? Find out who his family is. Where is he?'

'Who?'

'What the hell is wrong with you? Where is the dead man whose name you don't know?'

'Ah, right. Sorry, boss. Still at the front. In the medical room, presumably.'

'Okay, get him home first. We'll go out there tomorrow. Or the day after.'

'But, boss: five deaths in a month. It's urgent.'

'Let's let Willy stew a bit. He hates waiting. He hates unfinished business.'

Walker closed his eyes as a severe dizzy spell threatened to overcome him. He reached out with one hand and seemed to steady himself by leaning on thin air.

'Boss, we really need to get this interview with Ajok done.'

'Fuck. Okay, let's do some blah blah blah.'

Hail opened the door. 'Sorry, Ajok, that was rude of me to ask you if the equipment was turned off.' He gripped her arm, briefly. She nodded her acceptance of his apology, although she would have preferred it without the touching.

'And we're sorry to hold you up,' Hail continued. 'Walker is ready now.'

Walker was already sitting on his chair, cameras framing him from six angles. Ajok took her seat and ratcheted up her smile, while her crew fussed about with the equipment.

'Okay?' she asked. One of the crew nodded.

'Good afternoon, fellow citizens of Rise. I'm here with our most esteemed guest, the great man Walker, for an update for the people before the peace talks. Good afternoon, sir.'

'Always great to be with you, Ajok. And there's no need to call me "sir".'

'Thank you. But tell me, sir, it's been another big year of warfare —'

'Capped off just a few days ago, if I might interrupt you, by "The Battle of Sergeant Sala", one of the great moments we've all had the privilege to feast on. I'd go so far as to say it was better than "The Battle of Trench 21".'

'That's a big call, sir.'

'And one that I stand by. But you're right. Of course you are. It's never about one film. It can't be. I've been so delighted by the quality of the battles all year, and, if you'll permit me, I'd very much like to take this chance to thank all the committed soldiers — those fighting for the present and future of Rise, of course, but also our honourable enemies from Shine, led by the great Barton. You give all of us life. You make all of us proud.'

'And here we are again: another year gone, and another round of peace talks are upon us.'

'It seems like only yesterday that we wrapped up last year's talks.'

'What do you expect this time around?'

'Well, of course, when it comes to matters of specific areas of dispute and tangible progress, I cede the floor to our honourable Mr President, who I'm sure would be delighted to update you in exquisite detail. Such a way with words, that man. I truly envy him. But to answer your question to the extent that I can … it's okay, I can see from the way your eyebrows are dancing that you think I'm avoiding the question. From my perspective, the people of Rise want stability. In my opinion, we love stability. Always have, always will. And what's not to love? Stability is so sturdy. Yes, there are certainly some issues for the presidents to work through in the peace talks, but I'm hoping for more of the same over the next year. We have non-negotiables —'

'What are they?'

'Two full and fabulous meals a day, morning and night, for starters. Sure, we can't have a Sergeant Sala moment every day, but our bodies need regular fresh footage.

Our scientists, working closely with their counterparts in Shine, have proved that it's good for us all — and it's absolutely essential for growing children.'

'And so there is not any prospect of peace this year?'

'I didn't say that. The people of Rise crave peace. I personally crave peace. It's all I've ever wanted. I dream of peace every night. Ah, there's that exasperated smile again. Okay, I'll answer your question: everyone wants peace, nobody wants war, and we will deliver peace, one day soon. Very soon. I'm certain of it. Will it be this year? All of us will have to wait and see. But I'll tell you this: we have orange skies every morning, we have purple skies every night. We have each other. We have life, and life is precious.'

'Thanks be to Walker.'

'And thanks be to Barton. Never forget Barton. Great to see you, Ajok. Keep on smiling.'

* * *

Ex-Sergeant Sala, now simply Sala, chose the air train's last carriage. It was empty when she entered it, but, in the minutes before the train set off, it quickly filled with curious and thankful citizens. No one tried to speak to her or sit in the empty seat beside her. No one stared at the collapsed side of her face, the skin permanently mauve, an earlobe missing, half her nose shoved atop the other half.

The train simply took off, all heads facing forward. People just wanted to share the same space, the same air, with Sala. They wanted to feel her spirit. She understood this, and, although she preferred solitude, she did her best to enjoy the moment and to embrace the communality. It wasn't the same as going to war. Not even close. But it was something.

The train blew out to the fringes of Rise, every seat but the one beside Sala taken. Only on the return leg did people begin to dribble off, station by station. And when Sala reached her stop, she got off too.

A train trip — different routes, different people — became part of her daily routine. A carriage of humanity, silent but for the breathing.

* * *

The armoured vehicle — an Old Time troop carrier, renovated and sporting a new set of redundant wheels — carried Walker, Hail, and Curtin through the city of Rise via a private road that had once been a majestic winding river, the centrepiece of the old city. As word spread that Walker was on the move — he had to be, because no one else ever used this vehicle or this plastic-brick-paved road — people rushed to wave, cheer, or clap. For many years, Walker had actively discouraged such adulation. He had found it distasteful. Demeaning. Unhelpful to the cause. Pandering to the very excesses of the Old Time that caused the mess in the first place. But despite his misgivings, he'd always waved back and very often stopped for a chat. In time, he'd realised that the people weren't interested in turning him into some sort of god. They were grateful. They were friendly. They were alive. That was all.

At the city centre, they became a mini parade. The vehicle's rear door slid up, and Walker positioned himself in the opening. When someone started singing 'Let's Be Tender', Walker banged on the side of the vehicle. The driver eased to a stop, and Walker hopped down.

'Oh my fucking God, no,' Hail groaned. 'Not today.'

The whole crowd, and Walker too, belted out a spirited rendition of 'Let's Be Tender', including the rarely used fourth verse.

Hail stayed in the vehicle, poised to jump forward and prop Walker up should dizziness overcome him.

Curtin ignored it all, turned on a personal autoscreen, and worked on her analysis of the previous month's data on the strange illness, Walker's illness, which was continuing its slow random spread. She flicked open a map of Rise. Dots and splotches, but no pattern that either she or the computer could detect. She flicked the map to Cleave, with a quickly typed message: 'Any thoughts?' Bloody Cleave. This wasn't her thing — a current-day situation in Rise — but Curtin knew she'd have insights if she would just bring herself to leave the world inside her brain for a few minutes.

Walker, meanwhile, clambered up the embankment

to shake hands and slap backs.

'We're fucked if he tries to come back down by himself,' Hail said.

Curtin grinned. 'Have a little faith,' she said.

'He'll suffer for this later,' Hail said.

'Yes, but they love him. And he loves them so much that he's willing to put up with a bit of adulation.'

'Any chance it might help his … hunger?'

'It's more likely to do the opposite.'

'Great. What if we staged an incident? Someone fitting and foaming at the mouth, maybe.'

'You do that most mornings. It doesn't seem to help.'

'Find Walker,' Hail said into his wearable. 'Hey, boss, can you hear me? We need to get out to Grand Lake. Remember: five deaths?'

'On my way,' Hail heard in his earpiece.

'Need a hand getting down?' he asked.

'Definitely not. Watch this.'

'Oh no,' Hail said. He looked out the back of the vehicle just in time to see Walker jump from the top of the bank. It wasn't graceful, exactly — his feet hit the plastic with a jarring thud — but he stuck the landing. With a final wave to the people, he ignored Hail's outstretched hand and hauled himself back into the vehicle. The door closed, and he sunk to his knees.

'You're a fucking id—' Hail began, but Curtin interrupted him.

'Shhhh,' she said. 'Not now.' She crouched beside Walker. 'Follow my breathing,' she murmured. 'In … hold … hold … now out. In … hold … hold … out. Can you hear me? Out … Good. Again. Again.' She held his wrist to try to arrest the shaking that was passing through his whole body.

'I'm fine, I'm perfectly fine,' Walker said weakly. 'Perhaps I shouldn't have sung that song, that's all.'

'It's your song,' Curtin said. 'You had to sing it.'

Curtin and Hail helped Walker to a bed, bolted to one side of the vehicle. He closed his eyes and violently dozed as they passed through the flat districts of Rise and into the war zone of Grand Lake, the soldiers of both sides pausing a battle scene to allow them to pass.

Only when they reached Holland's command post, twenty minutes past the battle location, did Curtin give Walker's shoulder a nudge. He woke immediately, and Curtin had to hold him down. It didn't take much: just her palm sitting on his air-puffed chest. She inserted a probe up one nostril and read the information that appeared on a private autoscreen in front of her eyes.

'Better than I expected,' she said with a grunt. 'Not great, but good enough. Can you stand?'

'Are we there?'

'We're there.'

'Then I can stand.'

'Slowly, please. I said, slowly.'

They dropped the ramp this time, and Walker allowed Hail to take his elbow. But as Hail started moving them towards the buildings, Walker motioned for him to stay.

'I'll take care of this by myself,' Walker said. 'You two wait here.'

'Fine by me,' Curtin said.

'But, boss, there are all sorts of implications, complications. Don't you think it would be best if we confronted him collectively, if we —'

'I said, I'll do it.'

'Be careful. Don't forget it's Holland we're dealing with here. He's smooth. He's experienced. Why don't we just tag along. Even if we're just listening, hovering, it might help when we debrief back at the —'

'I. Will. Deal. With. This. Myself. Have you got that? Are you hearing me? Yes?'

'Yeah, yeah, I hear you, loud and clear.' Hail glanced up, saw the look on Walker's face, and pulled himself straight. 'Yes, boss,' he said, and remained erect until Walker turned, with a nod and the barest hint of a smile, towards Commander Holland, who had come out of the main building of the Active War Office and was waiting.

'Greetings, Commander Holland,' Walker said as he approached.

Holland stood to attention. 'Hello, SIR. It's a pleasure to see you, SIR. As always, SIR.'

'At ease, Commander.'

Holland ushered Walker into the building, a sleek all-plastic construction. The compound, over three decades ago, had started with a couple of huts, the stone salvaged from a restaurant that had sat at the water's edge for 130 years and had burnt when the first of several wildfires blew through. The original structures still stood, buried within the cluster of additional buildings that had appeared piece by piece as the enterprise of making war, and filming war, had become more and more sophisticated. They had everything they needed out here, even a cafe that served all the films they'd ever made. And they had their own mini domefield for when it rained.

Once Holland and Walker were inside, they dropped the formalities.

'How you doin', big fella?' Holland said with a grin.

'I'd be a whole lot better if you'd stop killing your people off.'

They embraced. Walker tried to remove his belly from the hug but only partially succeeded.

'Putting on a bit of weight there, eh? Big fella getting bigger?'

He reached out to give Walker's gut a rub, but Walker grabbed his wrist.

'Whoa there. There's only so much "at ease" a man can take.'

'Your little entourage not joining us?'

'Not this time.'

'But Hail never leaves your side these days. That's the word on the street.'

'When's the last time you spent any time on "the street"?'

'If you ask me, it's very sweet, all that devotion.'

'Well, no sweetness today. It's just you and me.'

'Alone at last. And still you won't let me give you a tickle.'

'Now, listen: what the fuck's going on?'

'What can I say? A run of bad luck, nothing more.'

'There's no such thing as bad luck. You taught me that.'

'I was young and foolish then.' He grinned, but Walker didn't return the grin. Suddenly, Walker was worried; suddenly, he smelt the impossible: treason. The Holland that Walker knew would not make light of the pain and suffering of others. He would not make a joke about the end of a human being's life. Walker had always thought that Holland's problem, his principal flaw, other than worrying too much about the flop of his hair, had always been his inability to cast aside worry and responsibility. He was a great commander precisely because he valued life so much. But it also made him relentlessly anxious. He'd never been able to let the pain of others go, to move on to the next thing, and the next, and in recent years the fretting had calcified. Many times, Walker had urged him to find a way to let awful but necessary moments go. This new behaviour of Holland's — this flippancy —

was not only out of character. And shocking. It was also, Walker instantly knew, fake. Something else was going on, something that Holland wanted to keep secret.

'Okay, okay,' Holland said. 'Look, about last night: the guy must have had a dodgy heart. How the hell was anyone supposed to know that, when he obviously didn't know it himself?'

'Was he up to date with his physical testing?'

'Oh, be fair. I feel bad, of course I do, but let's not descend into micromanaging.'

'Was he up to date?'

'Yeah, more or less. But shit happens.'

'More or less? Shit happens? Shit happens once. Maybe twice. Not five times. And not after a soldier has had his physical.'

'Those things aren't failsafe.'

'That's exactly what they're supposed to be.'

'People die. Accidents. Natural causes. Misadventure.'

'Not in this war, they don't. And they can't, not in these numbers. That's the whole fucking point. And it's your job — it's the most important part of your job — to make sure of it.'

'But each individual death is unrelated. There's no pattern, or none that I can see.'

'That's what the official investigation will determine. I'll need your report within a week. Sorry, Willy, but we're not going through the motions this time.'

'I understand that it's serious, but now that it's happened —'

'Now that it's happened five times in —'

'— now that it's happened, we'll probably go five years without any sort of incident. Let's put a bet on it. Come on: if I win, I get to give you a tickle. If you win, well, there's nothing you need, but you'll have the pleasure of victory. Yet again.'

'Fuck, Willy. This isn't funny. Five bodies in a month. Even if I wanted to let it slide — and I don't — I can't.'

'A month and a bit.' He saw Walker's face. 'A month and a bit, SIR.'

'No, that's not good enough. Not even close. There's a flaw in the system, a flaw in the personnel, a flaw somewhere with someone. I'd rather you find out what, but if you can't or won't I'll give the job to someone else. We run a clean show here, as you well know. We have to. No lies. Not amongst ourselves, anyway.'

'Full disclosure, warts and all: you're famous for it. But that's exactly why —'

'We're life-affirming, for Chrissakes. If we don't keep it clean and healthy, everything will fall apart. Everything.'

'— that's exactly why the people will understand a little slip, quietly dealt with, quickly forgotten.'

'Not everyone believes we're still on the right path. Not anymore. You must have heard rumours. Rumblings. Even out here.'

'Of course I have. But it's just a few crazies, surely. And it's idle chatter. It's not like anyone's going to storm Walker Compound, waving placards. Why not just ignore them?'

'I can't say I approve of the use of the term "crazies" for any of our fellow citizens.'

Holland came to attention. 'Quite right, SIR. Apologies, SIR.'

'Public opinion is somewhat delicate at the moment. It's … I can't tell you what it is, but take my word for it, five deaths in a month is not going to help at all, if news leaks out, and it's already leaking out, and —'

'A month and a bit.'

'Stop that now.'

'This level of caring: no wonder you're getting so fat.'

'And this lack of concern: you'll wither away. Look, it's your job — hell, it's your responsibility — to find the problem and fix it. The truth is, you should have sorted this out weeks ago. Surely you know that.'

'Sorted what out, exactly? You and I both know that this is part of war, always has been, always —'

'Sort it out, I say. Sort yourself out. Right? RIGHT?'

Holland reared back, shocked by Walker's ferocity. 'Yes, sir,' he said in a meek voice. Walker nodded and left the hut. Once the door closed behind Walker, Holland murmured, 'What I'm doing, I'm doing for you.'

In the time it took for Walker to walk from the hut

to the vehicle, his whole body had begun to shake. Curtin laid him on the mattress.

'Hold his head,' she told Hail. She massaged Walker's pulsating calves. 'Close your eyes,' she said to him. 'Focus on nothing. Relax your limbs. Relax, I say. Drift off. Come on, you can do it.'

'Isn't there something we can do for him?' Hail said.

'Find him something to eat. Something that he can stomach.'

'But nothing else?'

'Nothing that he'll ever agree to,' Curtin said. She unzipped Walker's shirt and got to work with antiseptic powder, muscle pushes and stretches, and warm words. Walker lay dazed, enduring her efforts. It was his head, this time, that had done him in, so light, so heavy. Only when Curtin pressed her palms gently against his temples did he begin to come back to himself.

'I'm so hungry,' he mumbled.

'I know you are,' Curtin said.

'But you've got more important things to do than fix me up, day in, day out.'

'I know I do.'

***

Flake kept up appearances, but everything was different. One day, he took a long detour on his way home from work — a sub-branch of the Institute of Peace Studies — to visit a shuttered shop on an alley in District 17, the seedy side of town, where the wind sometimes blew dust storms in from the fields around an airport from the Old Time. He greeted the shopkeeper, a bald man with sagging earlobes, with a nod. The shopkeeper ignored him.

'It's my first time here,' Flake said, almost in a whisper. 'I don't know what to do.'

'What do you want?'

'Photographs.'

'I can't hear you.'

'Photographs. Paper photographs.'

'Photographs — of course you do. Take Booth One. Voice-activated. No charge for looking if you buy, but charges start by the minute if you don't buy, with a minimum of five minutes. And close the curtain. I don't want to have to watch you.'

What a poor man, Flake thought, to be so unhappy in his work. He sat on a stool in a small dark cubicle and waited.

'Nothing's happening,' he called. 'Excuse me, but I need help. Nothing's happening.'

'I told you: it's voice-activated. You speak what you want.'

'Out loud?'

'You got a problem with that?'

'No, no, I … no,' Flake said. He almost stood and left,

overcome with embarrassment, shame, and shock at the shopkeeper's hostility. But he gathered himself and spoke quietly into the darkness. 'I want to see stills from "The Battle of Sergeant Sala",' he said.

An autoscreen appeared with a photograph of Sala's face, dirty but undamaged. 'No,' he said. 'Move forward. Post-recovery.' Images of Sala's damaged, healed face flicked before his eyes.

'Stop,' Flake said. 'That's the one. Oh my God, that's the one. But closer. Closer.'

A new image appeared. An extreme close-up of Sala's skin: red; smooth but bubbled. The image's resolution was extreme, and, to Flake's mind, magnificent.

'Purchase,' he breathed. 'Oh, yes yes yes, purchase.'

By the time he had gathered himself — patted his hair, wiped his hands on his pants, forced his breathing back towards an even state — the photograph, an actual image on an actual piece of paper that Flake could actually hold and touch, was waiting for him in a plain envelope. Even the envelope was thrilling.

Flake was about to flick his wearable across a reader to pay, but then he paused.

'Don't worry, Smarm-man: it'll appear on your bank account as Communication Maintenance,' the shopkeeper said.

Flake swiped the wearable and fled.

'You people disgust me. Such insolence: you might as

well be kicking Walker in the balls,' the shopkeeper called after him. 'Please call again.'

* * *

A few days after the visit to Grand Lake, Walker, Curtin, and Hail sat around Walker's private sitting area, the panoramic window giving them a view of Rise's night lights. Walker watched the video report on the life and death of Fred the dog — age approximately four years, vital organs misshaped and haphazardly connected to each other, the fifth leg a feat of nature (or, to put it another way, a consequence of Old Time shenanigans), the brain small but could have been worse — while Hail and Curtin engaged in cheerful debate about Walker's deteriorating condition, each of them implying that the other one could cure him if they only tried harder, cared a little more.

'I wish you wouldn't fight over me,' Walker said. 'It's demeaning.'

'You love it,' Hail said. 'But do you mind if I watch something, boss? I'm hungry.'

'You're always hungry,' Curtin said.

'I'm ravishing too, don't you think?'

'Do you two need to go somewhere more private?' Walker said.

'If only,' Hail said.

Curtin rolled her eyes, but Walker caught her suppressed smile. He knew, though they'd never told him outright, that they'd been together, sort of, up to a point, for years. They weren't a couple, which Walker understood: they were both too wedded to their own responsibilities, their own ways of being, their own painful memories, to fully come together. It was a common outcome for relationships in the New Time. Surviving came first, even once it seemed that survival might, just might, be a given. But Walker didn't understand why Curtin and Hail needed it to be a secret, except that Hail had strange ideas about protocol and believed that the abandonment of any principle of conflict of interest was at the heart of the Old Time troubles.

'Eat away, if you need to,' Walker said. 'It's no skin off my nose.'

'If only that were true,' Curtin said.

'Play raw footage,' Hail spoke into his wearable.

'You should watch too,' Curtin said.

'No point,' Walker said. 'No fucking point.'

'We've been over this: it's not "all or nothing". If you felt nothing, absolutely nothing, you'd have been dead weeks ago. Months. It's the same with the patients I'm monitoring. Which means there's hope.'

'Until there's not,' Hail said gloomily.

'I'd rather watch the lights than talk about this,' Walker said, but he adjusted his position so that he could watch the scene that appeared on the autoscreen that Hail had called up.

'This is from a few days ago,' Hail said. The footage was unedited, the offerings of a single camera, a drone hovering still, watching as three of Hail's finest stormed the enemy, inexplicably exposing themselves. They all went down in a barrage of plastic, but there was something staged — something overblown — about their assault, so obviously doomed to failure.

'That's terrible footage,' Hail said.

'They're overcompensating,' Walker said.

'You got that right.'

'It always happens after a classic moment. They'll have heard the reaction to "The Battle of Sergeant Sala". They'll settle down soon enough.'

'I'm surprised Holland didn't just order it deleted.'

'Not his job.'

'No, I know. But such poor work — it reflects on him.'

'He would never censor a battle. Anyway, wait for the edits. It'll turn out just fine.'

'Turn it off,' Hail said into his wearable. The autoscreen disappeared. 'What about the deaths?' he asked Walker. 'We should debrief, if you're feeling well enough. Did Holland's report have anything useful to —'

'We've lost him,' Walker said.

'No! We're talking about Holland. Are you sure?' Hail replied.

'Oh, he's got nothing to do with those deaths, nothing directly —'

'The most recent death was a heart attack, plain and simple,' Curtin confirmed.

'Such an unusual way to go,' Hail said.

'He had a little flaw in a chamber. He did 200 push-ups in four minutes. Boom.'

'Willy didn't kill anyone. Or let anyone get killed,' Walker said. 'But his attention isn't where it should be. And that's the point, that's the problem: he's as shifty as all hell about something. Telling jokes, for Chrissakes, about dead soldiers. *His* dead soldiers.'

'He's not himself,' Curtin said.

'Not that the jokes are funny: he hasn't got a funny bone in his body. And he knows —' Walker broke off to violently dry-cough.

'Do you want to lie down?' Hail said. 'Go to bed?'

'I'm fine.'

'Can't you do something?' Hail said to Curtin.

'He's just coughing. He'll be fine.'

'Thanks for your concern, doc,' Walker wheezed.

'Hey, you said it first. And the great Walker is never wrong.'

'What about Holland?' Hail said.

'Yeah,' Curtin said, 'give us some instructions in case you die in your sleep.'

'Also not funny,' Hail muttered.

'This is what we need to do: park a satellite right on top of his head. Tail him when he's off duty. I want dedicated officers on this. All day, all night. But go gently. Whatever he's up to, he's still our Willy.'

'Not Holland,' Hail moaned. 'Anyone but Holland.'

'Yes, I know. But it's not going to help if you take it so personally. It's the times.'

'You don't seem too surprised,' Curtin said.

'I always thought it was possible, right from the very start. He hankers for the authentic. That's why he's so good at his job. But there's only so much authenticity our little city can offer him.'

'Very deep, boss,' Hail said.

'Fuck. Off.'

'He's been doing it for too long,' Curtin said. 'We've left him there too long.'

'Probably,' Walker said.

'He's scheduled to take leave during the peace-conference ceasefire. Should we cancel it?' Hail said. 'Keep him in the field?'

'No, leave it be. I want to know what he gets up to on the home front. I mean it: twenty-four hours a day. Stick a probe in his ear and tell me what he's dreaming at night.'

* * *

Malee stood in the bricked courtyard of her tiny house, secure behind tall plastic walls. This was her haven. And this was the place, the only place, where she could heckle, out loud (though not too loud), as she watched war films two times a day. It was the only place where she could plot, in her singular way, a new future.

In the middle of Malee's courtyard, a single thin vine grew out of a scuffed black boot, an Old Time antique, the sort of suspect object that other people would have sent for destruction. The plant, neither sick nor thriving, had produced a single blue tomato, too small, too hard to bother picking yet.

Malee crouched down and took a vial of water, broke the seal, and dripped the water into the dirt inside the boot. She put the vial to her lips and sucked the last couple of drops of water. It tasted so sweet. So free. She sat on the ground and admired the plant, admired its fruit, admired her achievement in keeping it alive. Small steps: that was her way.

Suddenly, hooded figures came over the walls from all three sides, into the courtyard. Even in her panic, Malee recognised the dark-purple uniforms of Walker's military police. She turned to run, but a policeman stood in the doorway, barring her only escape route.

'But that's ... you're in my house,' Malee said. Before she could complain further, an officer placed a gag over her mouth.

'I do apologise for the intrusion,' the officer told her, 'but it's unavoidable under the circumstances. Let's not make a fuss or worry your neighbours.'

Malee pulled the gag free. 'You're worried about my neighbours? You're the one who just jumped in through their yards,' she said.

'We're not here to hurt you. We wouldn't dream of it. But I do respectfully request that you do what we ask you to do.'

With a nod, Malee repositioned the gag over her mouth herself. Although she liked to dream dissenter dreams in her wilder moments of fancy, deep down she believed in Walker's mantra: politeness, always politeness; mutual respect; a keen awareness that anyone around you could be experiencing a moment of memory-grief; and transparency. If she could have, she would have made her skin see-through: here I am. She only hoped that Walker and his purple police really and truly believed in these things too.

The officer clipped one end of a plastic chain to his belt and the other around Malee's wrist. Together they went up and over the back wall. Malee found the sensation of momentarily losing her stomach quite fun. But she wondered why they couldn't have left through the front door, given that some of the officers had apparently come in that way. She hoped one of them had thought to close the front door behind them. Crime was almost non-existent in Rise, but she didn't want her little house exposed to every passer-by. As she and her captor went over the wall, just before they dropped into the alley and the waiting windowless white van, Malee let the empty water vial slip from her fingers and drop to the ground.

Another purple officer grabbed the plant, boot and all. And then, as if they'd never been there at all, the courtyard stood empty. Peaceful. After a moment, though, a single hooded purple figure vaulted back over the wall, grabbed the empty water vial, and disappeared again.

None of Malee's entourage spoke, either to her or to each other, as they sped towards the far edge of Rise. Their destination was as close as they could get to the Grand Lake area without actually leaving the city. At the entrance to a large property — a sign that read 'SPARE PARTS' stood adjacent to imposing gates — the van entered a tunnel and came up in a vast compound, an anonymous prison hidden in plain view.

A man dressed in grey pants and a grey shirt took ownership of Malee. He was too tall for his own good, she thought. And unpleasantly handsome. He nodded a welcome but said nothing. She chose to match his silence as he scanned her eyes into the system, removed her wearable, and slipped a tracking device into the soft skin behind her ear, nudged up against a gland.

The door opened. A woman entered.

'Thank you, Leech, that'll be all for now.'

The man nodded to the woman and then to Malee, then left.

'Don't mind him,' the woman said. 'He's very shy. Especially around women. I tell him it's rude, but he's working on it. He's doing his best. Welcome to Spare Parts. My name is Gaite. I suppose you'd say I'm in charge around here. I wanted to apologise in person for any heavy-handedness. We aim to keep things simple. And quick. And pain-free. By the way, could I ask you to take your clothes off and put these on?'

She handed Malee a pair of grey-purple overalls. Malee undressed and dressed quickly. The prison garb was loose-fitting, soft, and surprisingly comfortable.

'Good,' Gaite said. 'Rest assured, we will treat you well. We are all friends here. I insist on it. Do you have any questions? You are free to speak, now or at any time.'

Malee really wanted to know what was going to happen to her clothes — especially her faded blue shirt, which she always wore when tending her plant — but she chose to stay silent. She wasn't scared. She'd always assumed this moment would come: Walker was benevolent, but he wasn't complacent. And he had eyes everywhere, human and robotic. She could have done without the gag in her mouth and all the flying about on ropes — they could have just knocked on her front door and she would have gone with them without a word of complaint — but she had no reason to doubt Gaite's promise that they would treat her well.

'Nothing to say?' Gaite asked. 'No questions? No complaints?'

Malee shook her head.

'But you're okay? Your wellbeing is most important to us. You'll tell us if something is troubling you?'

Malee nodded.

They put her in a cell by herself: tasteful pale-grey plastic tiles for walls, a thin but comfortable mattress protruding from one wall, a desk, a decent chair. An autoscreen listed the books she could call up. It was okay. She'd seen worse. She could live with it. She could live *in* it, for as long as she had to. That's what she told herself.

She'd been sitting there a couple of hours, not doing anything but feeling her way into the room, turning it into her space, when a voice — Malee recognised it as belonging to Gaite — crackled through speakers she couldn't see.

'Dinnertime, ladies and gents. Enjoy.'

A battle scene appeared on the autoscreen. Malee walked from the chair to the mattress. She lay down, face down, her hands covering her ears, but she couldn't block out the sounds of the battle scene. As her mattress vibrated to the sound of gunfire, she ate, and ate well. Oh well, she thought: it wasn't as if she had been planning a hunger strike. Death was not on her agenda, and neither, really, was a futile display of dissent. Except that, then and there in her cell, when the battle scene finished and the credits rolled, she found a use for her voice.

'Try a little patience,' she sang, as loudly as she could manage while staying in tune (she respected the song, after all). 'Try a little hope. Try a little light relief. Try a little belief. Try a little longing. Try a little tenderness.'

Gaite's voice came over her speaker, adding pleasing harmonies ... or trying to drown her out.

'Let's be TENDER. Let's be TENDER. Try a little TENDERNESS,' Malee and Gaite sang together. In the silence that followed, Malee sang it again to herself, in the privacy of her own head. This will be my song, she told herself.

**

Walker staggered to his bed and collapsed, half on it, half on the ground. Excruciatingly, he pulled himself fully up onto the bed and unzipped himself, freeing his belly. Almost immediately, he fell into a painful, fitful sleep: but he couldn't keep it up. In the middle of the night, he called for Curtin, who rubbed his arms and legs and belly, sprayed powder on the worst of the sores, and, despite Walker's groans of protest, ran a highlights reel of war footage on a loop, the autoscreen positioned at the tip of his nose. She sat with him until the robot parrot announced the day.

**

Sala gazed at herself in a mirror a moment longer before she walked out of the apartment, down the elevator, and into the bustling city street. After her decommissioning, which meant she'd also had to leave her Grand Lake outpost, she'd chosen to live in the very centre of Rise, towards the top of a tall building, surrounded by the din of humanity.

She walked slowly through the crowd, head held high. People stared, but most of them averted their gaze quickly, making a show of looking away, not out of embarrassment, not out of rudeness, but as a laboured mark of respect for her and the space around her. She felt herself moving within a bubble, even when bodies pressed close to her. She wondered if the bubble would always remain. She wondered if this was how Walker moved through the world. There was something odd about him — other than his fame. Not unpleasant. Not rank. But odd.

Sala entered the Grand Lake Bar, flicking her wearable at the door as payment, and sat on a stool. She called up that day's *Rise Times* on an autoscreen. It was full of news about the coming peace talks: fluff, she knew, as surely everyone knew. Usually she chose the written version of the *Rise Times*, but today she turned the speaking version on, letting Ajok's face, her prodigious smile, her trustworthy because familiar tone, invade her space. Around her, the bar's multiple screens, some public, some positioned for the benefit of specific patrons, ran a selection of muted battle scenes, new and old. Although she paid the screens little heed, she found the presence of the battles around her comforting. Warming.

But then, directly in her line of sight, her own image appeared on a screen, crouching behind that rock. The barman caught her eye and shrugged an apology. She rewarded him with a misshapen smile and could see that he was touched. Just for a moment, she felt the membrane of her bubble of isolation stretch thin. If she wanted this bar to be her local, and she was pretty sure she did, then she knew she'd have to put up with seeing herself on a screen from time to time. So long as they kept the sound down, so long as they steered well clear of close-ups, she had no complaints. She thought of the legendary Cleave, who, or so the story went, couldn't bear to be around other people. Sala understood the compulsion. But in the end, she didn't want to be isolated.

By now 'The Battle of Sergeant Sala' was showing on three different screens, and she had the whole room's rapt attention. Nobody approached her until eventually a bloke hitched up his pants and walked over.

'May I join you?' the man asked.

Sala sized him up: well-dressed, handsome in a look-at-me sort of way, tall if you included his pumped-up hair.

'Sure. Whatever,' she said.

'My name's Fry.'

'Uh-huh.'

'And you are? … Well, never mind, I know who you are.'

'Right.'

'So … um …' He strained for something to say, the moment altogether too momentous for him. 'Seen any good films lately?'

After a long pause, during which Sala stared straight ahead and the man had the decency to look appalled as he looked past her to the footage of her face exploding, she burst out laughing. Fry was encouraged.

'Do you want to get out of here?' he asked.

'I believe I do.'

Sala stood to leave. Fry pushed back his chair, but she extended her hand, making a stop sign.

'Yeah, fair enough,' he said, as he sank back onto his stool. At the door, Sala paused to flick her wearable over the reader.

'No, it's on the house,' the barman called. 'You're welcome here any time.'

She nodded. His appreciation was without motive, she could see. That's what she'd signed up for when she joined the army: to serve the people in exactly this way. As Sala left, Fry belched, quietly and not too unpleasantly, and wandered back to his bar stool.

'You're an idiot,' the bartender said, slapping him across the head in a friendly sort of way.

'Put her back on, will you,' Fry said. 'The whole thing. From the start. Every screen.'

'Four screens maximum. You know the rules.'

'Any chance of a close-up?'

'Hey! We'll have none of that sort of behaviour in here. Keep it clean or piss off.'

'Fine. Fine.'

Everyone in the bar switched their attention to 'The Battle of Sergeant Sala', prepared for her to feed them all over again.

***

Midmorning, later that week, Walker sat stiff in an armchair in a room in Walker Compound, so bored that he was willing to expose his belly and faint in plain sight if it delivered him from President Heelton, who sat opposite him, talking talking talking, on a straight-backed chair. A perfectly useless low table — what someone from the Old Time would have called a coffee table — sat between them, giving Walker a modicum of distance and protection from his chief talking head. Hail sat in the corner, observing through gritted teeth but not participating, just the way he liked it. Curtin paced near the door. Walker had complained that Hail and Curtin were making themselves too conspicuous, following him everywhere like he was a toddler. Even Cleave had commented on it, from her isolation. But Curtin was adamant: no chaperones meant no public appearances.

She was tired and worried: she'd worked all through the night, yet again, and when Walker had roused himself after a terrible few hours — when that damned mechanical bird he loved so much had started flying about, causing mischief — she'd been pleased but aggrieved that he seemed in such good spirits. As Heelton droned on, she leant on the plastic wall and closed her eyes, just for a moment. She had so much work to do. The eating illness was moving quickly from aberration, frightening but isolated, to a fully fledged emergency. But she expected Walker to crash at some stage before the day was out, and maybe crash hard.

For now, Walker was getting on with business. 'I must confess, President Heelton,' he said, 'and I mean this with all due respect, I still don't know what you're asking of me.'

'Can I put it like this —' Heelton said.

'Put it however you like. But coherently, preferably. And in the fewest number of words possible.'

'In the great, big scheme of life, and taking into account all you've achieved, five deaths is only five deaths. Sure, I get that. I do. Don't think me an idiot. Don't think me —'

'Perish the thought,' Walker said.

'Don't patronise me. Please. Don't devalue me. Five deaths: sure, it's a glitch, nothing more than a grain of sand in the bigger scheme of survival. But what if this sand comes from the badlands, and what if it glows green in the dark, and what if we inhale it, or it sears our skin, and what if —'

'Green sand? From the badlands? Oh my.'

'— and what if it goes down our nostrils, our throats, works its way into our bloodstream, crawls about our insides like a, like a, like a —'

'All right, now.' Walker dared to glance at Hail, who was making every effort not to laugh. Curtin had her back to him, staring at a wall. Walker suspected she was listening to an audio report.

'I'm starting to wonder,' President Heelton said, gazing at Curtin's back, 'if you and your people — don't worry, I know I'm not one of *your people*, your *inner circle*, never have been, never will be — I'm wondering if your people are fully awake and paying attention. Are they?' he said, casting his wide eyes around the room as if addressing Hail and Curtin directly. Neither of them replied.

'Because if they're not, that's okay — well, it's not, it's not, it's not okay — but if your inner circle is losing its edge, or just plain losing it, and if there's anything you need to tell me, now's the time to ... tell me. Please, is there anything you need to tell me? Is there? Is there? Is there? Because, and I feel it's my patriotic duty to warn you about this, the people on the streets are talking about the five dead soldiers. Five in a month.'

'We haven't made an official announcement. We probably won't.'

'Well, exactly. I'm the poor sucker who has to pretend it's business as usual.'

'It *is* business as usual, so far as you are concerned,' Hail muttered from his corner.

'Thank you, Hail. I believe you are "observer only" at this meeting,' Walker said. 'The people are right to be concerned about the five deaths,' he said to President Heelton. 'But their concern will pass. It always does. And quite right too.'

'Not if there are more deaths.'

'True.'

'And not if the other stories take hold. Someone is spreading dirty rumours: traitors or thugs or swindlers —'

'Steady on: we're all friends here.'

'Wake up. They are collecting snippets of information and using them to make a brand-new picture. They're framing that picture and projecting it on the wall like it's something pretty, only it's ugly and rancid, isn't it? Isn't it? I'm here to help, if only you'll let me. What do you need me to say? A straight rebuttal? A warning? Tough love? Tell me what tone to strike. Tell me what lie to tell, if that's what's needed. I'm speaking plainly now.'

'I hadn't realised.'

'Plainly, but metaphorically.'

'Okay.'

'I love you —'

'I don't know what to say.'

'— and revere you. And I know, believe me I know more than anyone else in this whole damned city, what you've done for us. All of us. And what you've done for me. Personally. But the rumours.'

'It takes you a long time to make your point, doesn't it, Mr President?'

'That's my job. But have you been listening? Have you heard my words?'

'Oh, I heard them. I heard every single one of them. Including the ones where you offered to lie to the people.'

'Only if it's necessary. Only if it's what you want.'

'It's not.'

'I was expressing my willingness, not my desire, to lie. I lie for you most days as it is. You must know this.'

'I've heard everything you've said, but I'm still waiting for you to say what you really came here to say, if indeed you came here to say anything. So, please, keep talking. We've got all day, all month, all year, I imagine, for you to find a way to plainly speak your mind.'

'Very well: I've heard rumours —'

'So you said. Several times. There are always rumours.'

'Rumours about ... Well: specific rumours. I'm sure you know what I'm talking about.'

'Thank you for telling me what I know.'

'Please don't make me repeat the rumours out loud.'

'Believe me, I have no wish to make you do anything you're not comfortable doing. Not now. Not ever.'

'Fine. I'll just come straight out and say it.'

'All right, then.'

'I'm talking about strange illnesses, people wasting away, people disappearing. I'm talking about seeds, water — water, for goodness sake — trading on the black market. I'm talking about people out there trying to grow plants: that's what I'm hearing, and if I'm hearing it, then I'm sure others are hearing it, and if others are hearing it, then I'm sure you're hearing it. Are you hearing it? Are you? These people hope to eat these plants. To eat them, for goodness sake. Only yesterday, my daughter asked me what bread was. I felt obliged to tell her.'

'You should be pleased that she's so interested in history. The Old Time is not a dirty secret. It's where we came from. I, for one, remember bread with fondness. A baguette stuffed with roast pork, chillis, cucumber, carrot. A hamburger bun, sweeter than it had any right to be, seared on a barbecue to stave off staleness —'

'But she's only twelve years old, her innocence lost.'

'Chapatis — oh, chapatis.'

'I expect, soon enough, I'll be asked to comment about these rumours. On the record.'

'It won't be in any scripts we give you. Not yet. Probably not ever.'

'But I live in Rise, in the actual districts.'

'Your house sits within a ten-metre wall, doesn't it?'

'I speak to people, ordinary people, all the time.

Answer their questions. Shake their hands.'

'It's funny, isn't it, that all the rumours are about plants. I wonder why there aren't any rumours about people tucking into animals?'

'Oh my God. Animals? Animals? *Animals?* Surely not even the most extreme extremist would resort to such craziness. Touch them? Kill them? Eat them? It's dirty. It's unsafe. It's the end of everything.'

'It'd be just like the good old days: cut up a carcass, cook it, and chew and swallow.'

'How oh how did it come to this? How did we sink so low?'

'Chew and swallow … We're just reminiscing, aren't we? I remember my childhood with great affection, when I can control the sadness.'

'Yes, but people are beginning to say that anything is possible. This will embolden the disaffected. Embolden them, I tell you.'

'No,' Walker said. He'd had enough of Heelton. He was ready to move on with his day. 'The dissenters foresee the end of compassion. They believe we will no longer feel any tenderness towards our fellow human beings. They believe our hearts will turn to stone. And what's more, they have no imagination. They can imagine a potato, if they work hard at it, what it once meant to the human race. But they can't begin to imagine today's potato, a rock-hard disc grown in carcinogenic soil, the flesh laced with lead, the skin glow-in-the-dark. Lightly steam, eat, and convulse. Die in minutes if you're lucky, weeks if you're too stubborn to see reality.'

'Can I stand in front of a microphone and give the city that line? Are you authorising me?'

'Definitely not. But it's no line. It's the truth.'

'The best lines always are. I'm not nearly as stupid as you, as everybody, seem to think I am. I can't even have a private meeting with you,' Heelton said, waving towards Hail and Curtin. 'That's how important I am. And I know what people say about me. The jokes. Even I have a spy or two.'

'You shock me.'

'You mock me.'

'Mr President, you misunderstand my impatience. You have my complete confidence. If you didn't, I would dismiss you immediately.'

'I'm democratically elected.'

'Come now.'

'I know that I'm not the great Walker, but who is? I cannot stand before the people like you can and simply make them believe me. I stand up and I give my spiel —'

'Your spiel? Now *you* give yourself too little credit.'

'— and I look into people's eyes and I can see them thinking, "There must be something more." And I agree with them. There must be something more.'

'All right. Listen: you're right, things are … a little

complicated, a little different, at the moment. Ever so slightly tricky. But I need you to hold on. Hang tough. We must protect the majority, and so we will root out the dissenters.'

'And then?'

'And then we will treat them the way we treat all of those who are downtrodden or misguided: with compassion. You're worried about five deaths in a month —'

'And I'm worried that you're not worried about them.'

Walker slammed the table that separated them. Curtin turned her head, surprised. Walker tried but failed to suppress a wince. 'Of course I'm worried about them. Those poor people. Their poor families. Every life matters. But think about this: if five deaths is a problem, think about the backlash if we abandon people just because they have a view that is different to ours.'

'Yes, but —'

'We will sweep them up. This is strictly off the record, for now. Do you hear me?'

'I hear you.'

'Off the record. We will find them all. We will match stealth with stealth. If need be, we will break them, in our tender way. And then we will embrace them, because that is who we are. Our actions will show them the true meaning of empathy, misguided though their beliefs may be.'

'Yes yes yes, but I need a new script to tell that story. Your "off the record" words aren't —'

'When the time comes, and the time is not yet, you will say this: "A few of us will surely starve, just as a few of us will eventually grow tumours that will finish us off. But the rest of us will remain healthy and happy and will survive and prosper and grow old, or at least what these days passes for old." But now is not the time for you to speak publicly about all this. Not yet.'

'But when?'

'Perhaps soon. But if things go to plan, that day need never come.'

'You put me in an impossible position.'

'Yes, that's your job.'

'Please give me some new words I can use now. This week, for the peace conference.'

Heelton's face, Walker couldn't help but notice, had turned a shade of purple. Then again, he'd always had an odd complexion, something like a sunset out over the badlands. It wasn't unpleasant, and it was one of the reasons Walker had picked him for the job in the first place, for once you were gazing at his face it was very hard to look away. Mind you, over the years, his neck and shoulders had grown closer to his chin, as if his head might one day disappear inside his body.

'Okay, I hear you,' Walker said. 'I truly do. But I can't give you what you want, not yet, and I'm asking you to trust me. Look, we found a way to feed the people — all the people — because we remembered that people can feel the pain of others. Sure, one person can make a fuss — "I demand the right to eat a cow" — but —'

'Oh my God, a cow. Don't start talking about cows. All that fur. All that flesh. I don't believe they ever existed.'

'And, sure, it only takes a few people with a few cows to wreak a bit of havoc. But the majority still believe in me. The vast majority. They trust me.'

'Until they don't?'

'As it's always been. As it should be. In the meantime, we must hold the majority up. We must honour and protect them. It's up to us: you and me. Go to the peace conference and talk at length about your hopes for peace. That's not a lie. I do hope for peace. Every day. Every hour. But we're not ready for peace.'

'But if people begin to discuss it openly in the streets: "What is bread?", for goodness sake. In my own home. I plead with you: take this situation seriously.'

'Take it seriously? Take it seriously?' Walker shook his head in wonder. 'Watch and learn, Mr President.'

* * *

On the first full day of his annual leave, Commander Holland, dressed in civvies, took a train to District 87, on the far edge of Rise. He walked through a semi-abandoned area, the buildings ramshackle but functional, their Old Time facades touched up with plastic here and there. He used the hood from his jacket to preserve his anonymity. He didn't want an audience. He didn't want to do anything to attract the attention of the hungry, well-hidden surveillance cameras. But although he took precautions, he felt relaxed to be away from the relentless drudgery of the war.

Holland was pleased to see that the few people out on these streets paid no attention to him. He didn't suspect that he was being followed by a military police officer, an up-and-comer called Wedge, also dressed in civvies. Rather than sitting on the air train, announcing himself — the single carriage was near-empty by the time Holland got off — Wedge had tailed the train in a vehicle, an oldish model, well-worn, carefully chosen to blend in with the area.

Wedge knew he needed to be smart if he was going to stay undetected: tailing the great Commander Holland without giving himself up was surely the trickiest of games. Even as he hung back, waiting for Holland to stop loitering and to do something, to go somewhere, he was distracted by the need to navigate around the scattered pockets of people who lived all the way out here. Most of them made a show of moving away at the sight of him. None of them wanted to talk to the police or even be seen by the police, and although Wedge was dressed casually, scruffily, not a hint of tell-tale purple, it was nonetheless obvious to the people that he was officialdom of some sort. Wedge didn't like the way they made him feel like some sort of pariah. And their choices discomforted him. There was no need for them to be scratching out lives way out here, on the fringes of the city. Wedge knew the reason — they couldn't handle the grief, the loss: their own, the world's — but he didn't understand it. Why wallow? Why not embrace the continuation of life? There was a place for these people with everyone else. Wedge thought of the people of Rise as a heart muscle, beating steadily. For the life of him, he couldn't think why anyone wouldn't want that.

The only local who had spoken to Wedge at all, who had even deigned to look at him, directly in the eyes, was a woman. Wedge found it hard to tell her age or her state of mind, but he suspected she was, like him, a child of the New Time, with no memories of her own messing with her.

'You shouldn't be here,' was all she'd said.

There was nothing menacing in her tone or demeanour: she wasn't threatening Wedge. She was making a statement: *you are interrupting my apartness*. Such muddled behaviour, Wedge thought, to try to avoid unwanted attention but to be such a misfit as to invite it.

Although no other people spoke to him, he felt many eyes on him. If all those eyes were watching him, he worried that they knew who he was watching. Were any of them working for Commander Holland? Would they expose him? And perhaps it was his imagination, but he felt as if he could smell the badlands, not so far away.

He knew he was overthinking the assignment. Annar, his supervisor, was always telling him to relax. It was easy for her to say: she was sure of herself, her skills. She'd done it all before. But this was Commander Holland, after all, under suspicion for … who knows what? Maybe nothing: maybe Annar was testing Wedge, preparing him for higher duties. Or perhaps she was trying to teach him something. In his most recent performance review, she'd called him a sanctimonious little bastard. She'd said it fondly, but Wedge was still taken aback. Him? Sanctimonious? Sure, he was a plain speaker. But that could only be a good thing.

One thing Wedge was sure of: nobody could have legitimate business way out here. Not even Commander Holland. Wedge had allowed himself to drift so far back that he'd lost Holland, at least momentarily.

'Confirm location of the subject,' he murmured into his wearable.

In head office, in a building near but not within Walker Compound, Wedge's colleagues Bull and Boosie sat in a locked room watching Holland on multiple monitors, although 'The Battle of Sergeant Sala' also played on the bottom left screen, because Boosie just couldn't get enough of it.

'Street 17. He's sped up. You should too,' Bull said into his wearable to Wedge.

'Let him do it his way,' Boosie said. 'He's being furtive.'

'Trying to be,' Bull said.

'He's doing okay for a newbie, don't you think? For a high-flyer.'

'Guys, I can hear you,' Wedge said. 'Please. I know what I'm doing.'

But he was too far away when Holland stepped off Street 17 into a tiny alley, upped his pace, ducked into a covered walkway, and sprinted past several buildings until he came to a door made of tired, dry wood. He turned the original Old Time handle, slipped inside, and made his way along a plastic-lined corridor, sunlight peeking through a half-hearted roof. Through a doorway missing its door, he passed into a dust-filled yard and then the shell of a different building. Inside, he picked a route through a maze of passages until he reached a dead end. He pressed the palm of his hand on the wall in front of him. After a moment, the wall disappeared into the floor. When he stepped forward, the wall automatically rose behind him. A bank of lights illuminated a steep, descending staircase.

Wedge, meanwhile, had broken into a trot and then a run.

'Where is he?' he spoke into his wearable. 'Quick, give me something.'

But Bull and Boosie's monitors didn't penetrate past the entrance to the narrow lane. They moved from camera to camera, but nothing took them into that world.

'Fuckity fuck fuck fuck,' Bull said.

'It's all right. Don't panic. You're always panicking,' Boosie said. 'It's all good. Wedge, my lad, are you there?'

'I wish you wouldn't call me "lad". I'm not nearly as young as —'

'Try every door. But, you know, try to stay calm, if you possibly can. I'm sending the drone in now. Remember, you can't let the subject see you.'

'But what if I open a door and he's standing right there behind it?'

'Hang on, lad, I'm just juggling tasks here,' Boosie said. He spoke into his wearable: 'Central? Central? Listen, we've still got the subject but — what I mean is, we've lost him. But we've got him. We know where he's gone.'

'Sort of. Kind of. Maybe,' Bull added.

'It's just that we can't actually see him. Can you authorise a sniffer drone?'

'That's dangerous,' Bull said. 'It's fucking Commander Holland. He's probably wearing a sensor.'

'No choice, buddy. It'll be fine. … Yeah, immediately, please,' Boosie said into his wearable. 'Okay, thanks … You there, lad? The drone will be with you in a minute or two.'

'Please stop calling me that.'

***

While Wedge wandered about aimlessly, Holland reached the bottom of the stairs. A camera above the door blinked to life before homing in on his right eye. After a moment, the door slid open. Holland walked into a large room brilliantly lit by artificial lights. There were several doors dotted around. A thick bed of dirt, separated into squares by plastic paths, covered the floor. Out of the dirt grew rows of plants, bedraggled but holding determinedly to life.

Holland walked to a plant, its sagging stalk held up by a plastic stake. He scrabbled around in the leaves, found an ear of corn, and pulled back the husk just enough to reveal that most of it was yellow and near enough to healthy, apart from one end, where the last kernels were a lurid blue. Holland sniffed the corn deeply.

Another door opened. Holland's sister, Dinn, entered. He ran to her, and they embraced fiercely.

'How's Mum?' Holland asked, finally extricating himself.

'She says she hasn't seen you for months.'

'I've been in the field. She knows that.'

'She's too old for months. She's too old for days.'

'I talk to her whenever I can. She gets to see my face whenever she wants to turn on the autoscreen.'

'I know. But it's not the same.'

'Best I can do.'

'Yeah, I know.'

'How are her tumours?'

'They're fine. Why wouldn't they be?'

'But she's fine?'

'I told you already: she's fine. She misses you.'

'Jesus, come on, Dinn: what else did she say?'

'She didn't say anything else. You know how she is: why speak when you can think? She misses you. Okay? She worries about you. We all do.'

'She doesn't know about any of this, right?' Holland said, indicating the plants.

'She doesn't know. But she's Mum. So she knows. You know?'

'How's her hip?'

'I told you: she's fine. Her hip is fine. Her tumours are fine. Her big toe is fine. Her memory, unfortunately for her, is fine.'

'And the children? How are the children?'

'I wish you wouldn't call them that. They're adults. They're out in the city, doing their thing, living their lives.'

'And Dunk?'

'He's fine too. He thinks he's starting to go blind —'

'Oh no.'

'It's nothing unusual at his age, surely. Most of us don't have the sort of access to medics that you do. I guess we'll fork out for a new set of eyes when it comes to that. There's nothing much else to spend it on.'

'Does he know that you're … here? Doing this?'

'Of course not. He's the ultimate true believer. Mind

you, if he found out, he'd probably dob me in to you, given that he worships the ground you walk on. So I'm pretty safe, I reckon.'

As they talked, they moved amongst the plants.

'Where does he think you are?' Holland asked, crouching down before a saggy cornstalk.

'Jeez, Willy: he's my partner, not my keeper. He doesn't keep tabs on me. He wouldn't want to try.'

'Okay, okay: just asking.' He showed Dinn an ear of corn. 'What do you think?' he asked.

'Yes. That looks good. Let's take it.'

'What about the blue?'

'It's not unusual for this species.'

'How do you know?'

'I know. It's perfectly safe.'

'Appearances matter.'

'So says the maker of fake war.'

'It's not fake.'

'Well, it certainly isn't real.'

Dinn pulled a blade from her belt and cut the ear of corn free of the plant. She cut off the misshapen blue part of the ear and dropped it at her feet. 'Happy?'

'You sure the rest of it is okay? That it's safe?'

'Yellow, blue: it's all safe,' Dinn said. 'But that's the point: we get this one tested before we harvest the crop.'

Holland reached for the corn. 'Give it to me. I'll deliver it.'

'No.'

'It might not be safe out there.'

'Exactly: who are they more likely to be watching, you or me?'

'I'm trained. I'm armed, if it comes to that.'

'Yeah, well, five deaths in a month, you'd want to be armed.'

'A month and a bit. But that's classified. How do you know about —'

'You said it yourself: appearances matter.'

'Does Mum know about the deaths?'

'You're putting us all in danger, which is all the more reason for me to deliver the corn.'

'I've already talked to Walker about the deaths.'

'I bet you have.'

'He's not thrilled, but it's fine. I wrote a report.'

'Self-regulation — it's never failed us yet.'

'It'll blow over.'

'Like radioactivity?'

'It's just a run of bad luck.'

'Is that what you wrote in your report?'

'I would never put my people in danger.'

'But five? Five? Mum says she's going to ask you for the families' details, so she can send them sympathy messages.'

'How did she even hear about it?'

'Well, I certainly didn't tell her.'

'I thought you said she was fine.'

'She *is* fine. Normal people send sympathy messages. Messed-up people write reports about dead people to exonerate themselves.'

'Excuse me for not being a performer. I don't grieve the way other people want me to grieve.'

'Life is sacred. You've been fighting the war, or whatever it is, so long you've forgotten that.'

'If that was true, would I be here, doing this?'

'Mum thinks you're going to disappear. You know, be disappeared. She's not the only one.'

'No. That's not Walker's way.'

'Yeah, he's an honourable and humble man. If you really believed *that*, you wouldn't be here, doing this.'

'I've never said he was humble. God, *he's* never said he's humble. Why on earth would he want to be humble? Why would anyone?'

'You should watch your back. You need an escape plan.'

'I'm telling you, he'd never do anything like that. Not to me. Not after everything we've been through. And if he does — he won't, but if he does — I'll wear it. Besides, I've got nowhere to escape to.'

'Have you ever done anything you regret? To another person? In Walker's name?'

'What, I … why are you even asking me that? No! … Well, not for years. Not since the very early days. And never — never! — without a good reason.'

Dinn snorted.

'Do we have to talk about this now?' Holland asked.

'If not now, when? We never see you. We can hardly talk about it over autoscreen.'

'But, look, I've told you this so many times before. I can't believe I have to excuse myself again. We — Walker and Barton and all of us who followed them first — did what we had to do, for the good of those who could go on living.'

'Yes. That's my point. You did what you had to do.'

'He loves me. He's like my big brother.'

'Aww, shucks, how sweet. You should put that story up on the screen. Oh, how the peasants would feast.'

'It's true,' Holland said defensively.

'Jeez, I know it's true. But he's sniffing around you. I can see it in your eyes. We can't take the risk with the crop. And with God knows what else. You know that I'm right. Come on. It's time to move.'

Dinn pulled her shirt off and lifted her arms above her head. Though he was still reluctant for her to be the courier, Holland sat the corn against her stomach, placed a patch over it, and then taped the corn to her body. She put her shirt back on, embraced him briefly, and left. Holland gave the garden a last glance before heading towards the door he had arrived by. But then he paused. Dinn was right. He needed to be careful. More careful than he'd been so far.

He chose to leave by a different door, one that took him into a cool, musty tunnel lined with Old Time bricks.

Holland swept an autotorch before him, lighting the way, until he came to a dead end. He shone the light up and down. There was an Old Time metal disc embedded in the floor. He pulled it up, and stepped down a ladder into a vast tunnel, a long-abandoned Old Time train line. He began the long walk home, leaving Wedge behind a pile of rubble, waiting hopefully but hopelessly, muttering periodic updates — 'nothing to report' — into his wearable, while the drone flitted about, piecing together the story.

***

At the opening ceremony of the 33rd Annual Peace Conference, all eyes were on President Heelton of the city-state of Rise and President Rant of the city-state of Shine. Dressed in identical pale-brown pants and white tops to ensure equality, they walked together, hand in hand, through the assembled crowd to the stirring sounds of 'Let's Be Tender' as performed by a digitally produced 200-piece orchestra. They stood for footage beneath a giant banner that read 'PEACE: not this year, maybe next year'. Soldiers marched around them, children waved streamers, and the crowd cheered wildly and chanted, 'Not this year, maybe next year, not this year, maybe next year, not this year, maybe next year'. Just like the 32nd year, and the 31st, and the 30th, it was the best opening ceremony ever.

The opening ceremony was projected onto autoscreens throughout both cities: two laughing, smiling leaders, their relationship something more than chummy, something less than carnal. On a street corner, feeling exposed, feeling that he needed a decent clean, Holland stopped and watched Heelton closely. The man was smiling as widely as ever, and clapping and chatting and waving like he was supposed to, but Holland could see the tension in his frame. He'd seen something similar in his soldiers when they'd sensed — sometimes correctly, sometimes not — that it was their turn to cop an injury. They could feel a bullet coming, and with it, perhaps, the pinnacle and the end of a career. They kept their courage — after all, they were well-chosen, well-trained, proud — but they lost spontaneity in their movements, their decisions. And whenever Holland saw it, he gave them a break: a few days, maybe a week. Without fail, they came back stronger. But poor Heelton: he'd clearly had enough, and Holland had his doubts that any holiday would help him to come back stronger.

Holland transferred his gaze to the faces of the people standing around him in the street. Even after all these years, they were all gazing up, rapt. Holland found it incredible. These people weren't sheep. They were thinkers. Most of them were tough. And yet here they were, eyes upturned together. One old man's shoulders heaved as he sang 'Let's Be Tender'. Holland understood, better than anyone, or thought he did: Walker and Barton had saved lives. They'd saved all the lives. And so, after all this time, the people lined up to cheer a set of negotiations they knew were a sham. They were complicit, and good on them. Walker and Barton made the grand, radical, desperate experiment work. The wonder of it was undiminished, for Holland. But now it was time for change — Holland was certain of it — and the majority of the people weren't keeping up.

He looked back at the autoscreen. The presidents shook hands for over a minute, and cameras from all angles caught the moment for tedious posterity. Only then, with a final wave, did they leave through a set of doors, ornately decorated with curved lines of blue and red plastic.

* * *

Far away from the ceremony, Walker sat with Barton in the meeting room of Walker Compound. A short, muscular woman, Barton wore her hair bundled to one side, as if she wanted it well and truly out of the way. The true leader of the city-state of Shine, she was Walker's collaborator. His only true equal. Together, the two of them had found a way to survive the chaos and hopelessness of the Old Time. And then, understanding how they'd done it, they'd found a way to keep saving what was left of the world, day in, day out. Each of them had taken a city and declared a war of survival on the other.

Barton lounged in her armchair, her shoes thrown off, her calloused toes pointing to the ceiling. She watched the presidents shaking hands with a bemused look. She wasn't sure, five years in, that Rant was right for the job. He was fierce. Quick to anger. She didn't mind that — it was one of the reasons she'd chosen for him to win the election after President Vannland had retired. But Barton missed Vannland because Vannland had known, without ever needing to ask or argue, what Barton needed her to say. Poor Vannland: grief had got her in the end. It happened, Barton knew. She was surprised it didn't happen more often. She still hoped Vannland might rise again: a psychological recovery, a political return. But she doubted it.

Walker sat stiffly, partly because he ached all over — he had positioned himself as comfortably as he could, and was trying not to move — and partly because he was bemused by how relaxed Barton was. Sure, she always discarded her public persona when she was with him. Of course she did. But he couldn't remember ever seeing her bare feet. It was almost obscene. In the meantime, he wasn't ready to tell her his secret. Not yet, at least. The less he moved, he thought, the less chance there was that he'd faint or that the sore on his cheek would start bleeding.

'We need a couple of new editors, don't you think?' he said. 'The Sala film is a work of genius, but we need improved content, routinely, regularly — morning, noon, and night.'

'Straight to business, eh?' Barton said.

'Lots to get through.'

'Have you ever thought that you and I should have a parade to start our talks? It might be fun.'

'You have to agree: some of the battle footage through the August to October quarter was far too predictable. Ours and yours. And the rest of the year has only been marginally better. And the set designers need a shake-up. They got the placement of the rock in the Sala footage right, but there's been other times when —'

'Details.'

'Details matter. I'm pretty sure you taught me that. This notion that we can serve up the same dusty bloody hill all day every day just won't do. And as for —'

Walker paused mid-sentence as a wave of dizziness came over him. He gripped the armchair and forced himself to breathe slowly and evenly, as Curtin was always telling him to do.

'I heard you were struggling —' Barton said, in a matter-of-fact tone.

'You heard, eh?'

'— but I didn't know it was this bad. Why didn't you tell me?'

'It's just a dizzy spell. It happens to old people, I'm told. It's nothing to worry about. Give me a minute.'

'A minute? I can give you anything you want.' She paused and then winked. 'Anything at all.'

Walker lifted his head unsteadily. 'What's that supposed to mean? Don't tell me, after all these years, you finally want to fuck me?'

'I told you when we were sixteen, and I'll tell you again now: you're not my type. Especially in your current condition.'

'What's that supposed to mean?'

'It means that your makeup isn't quite doing its job. It's a miracle that nobody has twigged yet.'

'About what?'

'Oh, Sunil,' Barton said. Walker knew the game was up: Barton hadn't used his Old Time name in decades. Barton stood, hauled Walker to his feet, and unzipped his shirt. She rested one hand on his belly. Walker made no effort to stop her.

'Well, now,' Barton said. 'You should be dead.'

'You knew, eh? Hail been talking to you?' Walker asked.

'He didn't need to.'

'Did he tell you about the dog?'

'He didn't tell me, but I heard.'

'Spies in my midst, is it? Curtin? No, she'd never do that,' he said. 'Surely not Cleave?'

'You should have told me yourself.'

'I was … embarrassed.'

'Of course you weren't. You should have told me,' she said again.

'It helped, but only a bit. The dog, I mean.'

'Well, that's typical Hail, isn't it? Inventive but predictable; different but safe.'

'Safe? The damned thing glowed in the dark. And it slobbered.'

'Forget the dog.'

'I wish I could.'

'How about something entirely different: fancy some broccoli? How about a carrot? I might even grate it for you, if you ask me nicely.'

'What a kind offer. But I'll pass.'

'What about a bread roll? Pane di casa?'

'Don't you let dear President Heelton hear you talking like that. The very idea of it will send him into a panic: the corruption of our youth.'

'Well, it takes very little to scare your Mr President these days, speaking of people who need a shake-up. But perhaps in time he'll grow accustomed to the idea of bread.'

'Not in my lifetime.'

'Your lifetime? What are we talking? Weeks? Days?'

'On my watch, dear Prez Heelton won't care about the idle dreams of a tiny minority who, trust me, won't be around for long.'

'New ideas need time to settle, I see. Not unlike a bread roll in your Mr President's stomach.'

'Now who's light-headed?'

She took his shoulders and eased him back into his chair. 'Sit,' she murmured. 'Rest.'

'Ahhhh,' he muttered in relief. His chest heaved, once, twice, and then settled.

'Should I call for Curtin?' Barton asked. 'I'm sure she's close.'

'I'm sure she is too. But I'm fine. Lots to talk about. Lots to do. Anyway, she's busy. She's the busiest person in Rise.'

'I can't believe you didn't tell me it was this bad.'

'I knew that you knew. For a recluse, Cleave's an awful chatterbox.'

'I saw it with my own eyes. I heard it in your voice. Have you forgotten that I know you completely?'

'Well, there you go. That's exactly why no one else will ever notice. Because you see me, really see me, but you're the only one who does. The people — even Hail, even Curtin, even Holland — see what they expect to see. I could be dead and rotting and they'd still see me standing before them.'

'Maybe. Maybe not. Five deaths in a month rings alarm bells, even amongst the most apathetic, the most

118

convinced, the healthiest, the happiest.'

'That information is not public.'

'Sure, but everyone knows. Your most senior, most experienced, and most trusted commander, and yet five in a month.'

'Yes, yes, I know.' Walker sighed. 'Hail will have a fit if he sees me like this,' he said. He attempted to fix his shirt, but he couldn't manage it. Barton leant in, zipped him up, and patted him on the shoulder. He winced.

'What are we going to do about Holland?' Barton asked.

'Now who's all straight down to business? … He's my problem, I'll —'

'No, he's our problem now. Does he need a few months off? Is he sick? Is he slowing down? Does he need to retire?'

'I'm looking into it. Now. As we speak.'

'And?'

'And … I'm worried about him. Worried about what he's up to.'

'As you should be.'

'Is there anything about my city you don't know?'

'He's a symptom, I know that. A symptom of the big picture. Things are afoot.'

'Yes, I know. Pane di casa.'

'Pane di casa.'

'But we'll ride it out,' Walker said. 'We'll fight back

when necessary, quietly but firmly. We'll break the resistance, although they're so weak, so hesitant, so misguided that I hesitate to bother.'

'Fighting words from a dying man.'

'We'll do whatever we have to do to preserve our way of life. But we'll do it in our restrained way. Our compassionate way. We leave no one behind here, and —'

'I'm weeping in the face of your forbearance. Your dignity.'

'— and then, if and when we have to change the way we do things, we will change on our terms. We will set the timetable. Nobody else.'

And with that, Walker slowly slid from the chair towards the ground. Barton caught his face before it hit the plastic tiles. When she rolled him over, her fingers had branded his face. He was conscious, up to a point.

'Deep breaths, now.'

'Such useless advice. If I could brea—'

'In, out, in, out.'

'I can see clouds. Oh God, is it raining?'

'Keep your eyes open.'

'I can't.'

'This is Barton speaking,' Barton said into her wearable. 'Curtin? Is Curtin there? Put her on immediately … Is it you? … He needs you. Now. No one else comes in.'

'Here's a thought,' Walker murmured, 'what about we —'

'Shhhhhhh.'

'— we get President Heelton to defect to you. Then you can retire him. Do you have a house with a view for him?'

'Let's call it a day, eh? We'll talk more business tomorrow.'

'Why do the people give me more credit than you?'

'I really can't imagine,' Barton said. 'Now lie still.'

* * *

Dinn left her vehicle a few blocks away from her destination — a futile gesture of subterfuge, she knew, but it made her feel in control — and walked through the pristine streets of an inner district. She found it an effort to walk because she was so tense. Mostly, though, she was worried about Holland. She was almost certain that he was going to disappear, to die, or, at best, to end up in some anonymous prison for whatever time he had left. It was his own fault, in so many ways, Dinn thought. And she knew — oh how she knew — what a magnificent achievement it had been for the most dogmatic man left on earth to change his mind, to see that the new way now needed its own new way. But, even now, he continued to see the world through his old alliances and through the facts of his great achievement. She understood that too: Walker — no, Barton and Walker — had indeed saved them all. Saved humanity. And Holland had helped. But

121

that didn't mean that they were going to be right about everything until the end of time … the end of time again. She knew that Holland wanted to do what was right. He really did. But he wanted to do it without breaking any old bonds. Without rejecting his mentor, his hero, his great friend. Dinn couldn't see how that was going to be possible. She didn't even want it to be possible. All this friendliness, all this compassion: in the end, it grated.

She wound through streets and around vehicles and past people, checking frequently to see if she was being followed. She believed — or hoped, at least — that she was in the clear. But she wasn't. Wedge was there, closer than she could have imagined, bolder than he had been when he'd tailed Holland.

Dinn skirted down a laneway, narrow but brightly lit. A young man walked towards her. As they came together, they stepped into a doorway, facing each other. The man lifted Dinn's shirt, ripped the corn cob free, and handed it to her. He then lifted his own shirt, and she stuck the corn to his torso. They carried on walking, away from each other. Cameras followed them both. Wedge saw it all. He followed the corn.

* * *

The Grand Lake Bar was packed on the first night of the peace talks, the mood celebratory. Sala had to stand wedged between two strangers. Neither of them took advantage of their proximity to her, but one of them made little effort to give her more space and let his arm dangle loose alongside hers. Sala's friendly bartender chatted to her in between loading footage, the usual war scenes mixed with images of past peace conferences. He had a theory about a better type of domefield that he wanted to run by her. And he wanted to know if she'd ever met or seen or spoken to Cleave, because rumour had it that she didn't actually exist. Sala liked his banter, his easy friendliness, his lack of an agenda, but she could see he was run off his feet. She thought about asking him his name. Instead, she slipped away while he was pulling up vintage footage of the first peace conference. She walked the unusually busy night streets for a couple of hours before she went home. After 300 sit-ups, she finally pushed towards something resembling sleep.

Grainy lay strapped to his bed, force-fed battle scene after battle scene. He'd lost track of how many days he'd been here, and had no idea it was the first day of the peace talks. Some days, he thought he was feeling better. Other days, he was too tired, too sore, too hungry to even sit up. His mattress was in permanent motion, warding off bedsores.

Geraldina and Flake, like many people in the districts, sat on the ground in front of their house. They chatted with their neighbours, they watched the purple sky fade to black while the children fell asleep at their feet, they gave quiet thanks for another year, and they remembered their loved ones. They leant against each other and told each other that their tumours were stable, more or less, and that life was good and would be even better for the girl and the boy.

Malee sat in her cell, watching Ajok's report on the peace conference: good progress, positive signs, mutual goodwill, significant issues still unresolved. And lots of smiling.

'Play last year's footage,' she yelled into the chasm.

'Good idea,' said a voice over the loudspeaker. And straightaway, there it was: good progress, positive signs, mutual goodwill, significant issues still unresolved. And lots of smiling. Malee sat on her bed, waiting it out. 'Patience,' she told herself. 'Patience,' she yelled into the night.

***

Cleave sat in her private courtyard, smelling the air. As she pondered her ageing nose, an alert went off. It was Walker, requesting an urgent conversation.

'Why today? Why now?' she muttered to herself. She thought this every time he intruded upon her. She sent him information and advice constantly. He always wanted something more, something specific, something prosaic. Awful. Sometimes she thought she'd get more peace and quiet if she moved back into the main compound.

She turned on an autoscreen. Walker's face appeared. Devoid of make-up, it revealed his sunken eyes, his sore-infested cheek, his sparse eyebrows. Cleave didn't speak. She just looked.

'I've got something to show you,' Walker said. He took a few unsteady steps backwards and wrestled with the zip of his shirt. 'I can't do it,' he said. 'You need to help — can you help?'

Curtin came into shot.

'Hey,' Cleave said fiercely. 'That's against the rules.'

She disconnected the autoscreen and took several deep breaths. The air still smelt okay.

Walker buzzed her again, requesting another face-to-face meeting. She ignored him. A message came through: 'It's just me now. I promise.'

Reluctantly, she connected. 'How could you let that happen?' she asked. 'No one sees me but you and Barton. That's the agreement.'

'It was an accident.'

'No.'

'I'm not myself.'

'What's wrong with your face? You should clean it.'

He stepped back and allowed the camera to dwell upon his bare torso.

'Oh,' Cleave said. 'You've got it, then.'

'It's been a while. Months. But it's getting worse.'

'What's going to happen?'

'I'll die.'

'Who will I have to talk to then?'

'It'll be Curtin. Okay?'

'She asks me so many questions. She's always sending messages.'

'It's your job to answer her questions.'

'So many interruptions.'

'Things are changing. We're going to need you more than ever.'

'I work the way I work.'

'When it happens, when I'm gone, will you talk to Curtin? Face to face? Like you do with me.'

'I suppose I'll have to.'

'I suppose you will.'

***

Wedge, dressed in his purple uniform, and a small team of military police broke into the room where Holland and Dinn grew their plants. In haste, they installed hidden cameras. They found a pipe that supplied water and, careful not to touch the stuff, took a sample. Wedge donned gloves and carefully removed a selection of leaves from plants. As they departed, Wedge sniffed a sickish-looking tomato. Another officer grabbed him by the shirt and pulled him away.

'What are you doing?' the officer whispered. 'Those cameras are already live.'

* * *

At dawn the next day, Holland, disguised by his unshaven face lost in a hood, moved through the abandoned outskirts of Rise with an image of an Old Time map hovering before him. Soon enough, he found what he was looking for: an abandoned airport, outside the range of the domefield, the huge hangars perfect for a secret farm. He moved quickly from building to building. He could see it already. The next step. The escalation. They could convert the planes into sleeping quarters, offices, storage areas.

But the planes also shocked him: so well preserved, so forgotten but dangerously familiar. They needed a makeover — a plastic spray job, the wings detached, something, anything — or they would provoke grief and longing.

In one hangar, Holland disturbed a bedraggled group of people: two women and a few children of varying ages camping together, doing it tough.

'I'm sorry, but you can't stay here,' Holland said in a kindly tone. 'You're in an "off-limits" zone. Strictly military police only.'

'Don't see any purple on you, fella,' one of the women

said, hauling herself up. Strong legs, Holland thought. He tended to judge people by their soldierly traits. The woman folded her arms and silently stared him down.

'Did you hear me?' he said in the same kindly tone. 'You must leave. It's for your own safety. It's for the greater good.'

'The greater good?' the woman said.

'The greater good. We must all do our part.'

The woman took a couple of steps forward. She reached for Holland's face.

'Hey — back off. Back off now, or I'll be forced to take action.' He drew his gun but pointed it at the ground rather than directly at the woman.

'Oh, for fuck's sake, put that fucking thing away, you fucking fucker,' she said. 'What am I going to do, scratch your eyes out?'

'You just might.'

'Yeah, and you might kill us all without a second thought.'

'It's a stun gun. It'll give you a bruise, at worst.'

'I might hit my head on the way down. You'd leave me here to rot, you fucking fucking fucker.'

'What are you even doing out here? There's no reason for it. There's no need. There's a place for everyone in Rise, no matter what your feelings about the past —'

'You don't know a fucking thing about me, fuckface.'

'— no matter who or what you miss.'

'Hey, you look familiar.'

'It's grief, isn't it? Is that what's forced you to live out here? I understand, believe me, I do. I think about the Old Time constantly. The people I lost. That we all lost. But there are ways of moving on. Procedures, if it comes to that. I'd be happy to help. Think about it, for the sake of the children, if not for yourself.'

'I know you, don't I? I want to see your face. Show me.'

'No, I, stop that.' She came at him again, with her fists. 'Stop it, I say. Step back.'

'Show me or you'll have to kill me,' she said, pulling at his hood.

'Stun you.'

'I'm unstunnable.'

He gave her a shove, harder than he intended. 'All right,' he said. 'Stop. I'll show you.'

He eased his hood back. The woman looked hard at him, and glanced behind, checking the other woman and the children.

'I knew it,' she said. 'You're, you're, you're … you're that Commander Holland, aren't you? You're fucking famous.'

'Yes. Yes, I am. And might I know your name?'

'We are in the presence of a bigwig. A fucking saviour. Bow down, people. Genufuckingflect AND THAT'S A FUCKING ORDER.'

'Really, there's no need for —' Holland began, but, before he could finish his sentence, she hit him flush on the jaw. At the last moment, he had seen the blow coming. He'd chosen to stand still and accept it, not because he wanted this woman to hit him, not because he was being polite, not because it had been so long since he'd seen, let alone been the recipient of, such straightforward aggression, but because, although he could see that the woman didn't know it, he was probably on her side. She knocked him off his feet. She rejoined her group, and they shuffled away.

'You never told me your name,' Holland called out, dreaming of future recruits.

* * *

Fanfare heralded the second day of the annual peace conference. President Heelton and President Rant appeared, again, to music, flags, soldiers, children, and crowds. As they shook hands, pumping each other with great enthusiasm, banners unfurled that read, 'DAY 2: NO MEANINGFUL PROGRESS'. Autoscreens everywhere played the highlights of the previous year's fighting. A consensus seemed to have emerged: why mess with such a fine war?

* * *

'I'm perfectly okay now,' Walker told Barton, after they'd watched their presidents prance about.

'Sure you are.'

'Or at least well enough to talk. Come on — it's too important. We've got decisions to make.'

Barton wasn't convinced. Walker's face was grey and his eyes were yellow — and yet his gut, his collapse the previous day, had reinforced to her what she already knew: their whole grand, glorious enterprise was under threat.

'Okay,' she said. 'But I'm calling Curtin at the first hint of a problem.'

'She's hanging around outside anyway. Anyone would think she didn't have important things to do.'

'Let's not tiptoe around the problem: what are your latest numbers for the sick?' Barton asked.

'Curtin's got the detailed figures. Best we can tell, it's pushing 4,000. That's an estimate. We have evidence that some of them are keeping to themselves. Hiding in small groups, even. They have no idea what's wrong with them.'

'Ours is higher. Maybe closer to 5,000.'

'Well, your population is higher too.'

'How many dead?'

'Oh well, we keep most of them going, one way or another. The ones we know about.'

'Come on, how many? Are we having this conversation or not?'

'At last count, a couple of hundred, give or take.'

'That's an underestimate, surely?'

Walker inclined his head to the door. 'As I said, you'd

have to ask Curtin if you want a precise number.'

'So you're underestimating,' Barton persisted. 'Surely you want to know the exact number. Surely you *do* know it.'

'It's tragic. But even if I believed your numbers, which I don't —'

'You don't believe them or you don't want to believe them?'

'— either way, it's a tiny problem. I'm not being flippant: I don't want anyone to be sick. I mourn every death.'

'I know you do.'

'But our responsibility must be to protect the majority. The vast majority.'

'But the trend is upwards. Undeniably upwards.'

'Maybe.'

'There's no doubt: the people are losing their compassion.'

'If that's true — I'm not conceding, don't look at me like that — then we must do better. We must give the people new reasons to care.'

'Maybe. Or maybe there's nothing we can do about it. Maybe compassion has run its course. Maybe we need to change tack entirely.'

'Yeah, sure, let's reverse the last thirty years. Give in. Go back to the way things were. Magically return to the Old Time.'

'Maybe it's time for us to plan a new New Time.'

'Yeah, let's do that.'

'I'm serious.'

'No, you're not. You can't be. It'd be the … you'd be razing everything we've achieved. And you'd be insulting the memories of everyone who didn't survive. All of our loved ones.'

'Not at all, and you can take that disgusting suggestion and go shove it up your diseased —'

'Nothing personal.'

'You're a sanctimonious shit when it suits you. Especially when you're wrong. Look, we've always known this day might come. For goodness sake, we've prayed for it.'

'I don't pray. You don't either. There is no God. Not anymore.'

'Goodness, aren't you pent up today? Look, I'm sorry you're on your last legs, I'm sorry you can't feel anything for anyone, but it's not all about you and your fucking legacy. Maybe, just maybe, it's time to think about letting a little peace break out.'

'It's too soon.'

'"Not this year, maybe next year", eh?'

'It'd be a disaster.'

'Who for? You? Me?'

'Famine would rage.'

'I doubt it. But maybe. And maybe we need a small catastrophe to save us from a big catastrophe.'

'What do you want to do, start a revolution against

ourselves? Flick the switch for the extremists?'

'Isn't it better that we do it ourselves? We've transformed the world before, after all. We can do it again. Why force others to revolt when we can lead the revolt?'

'To test them. Their ideas. Their plans. Their infrastructure. Their leadership. Their courage. They are few, and they are weak. They will crumble. If they don't, fair enough.'

'Maybe. But their numbers are growing. Fast. We're tracking nine different groups in our sector.'

'Yes, I know all this. We have them too. We're monitoring them, dealing with them when necessary. Don't look at me that way: we're just giving them a little fright now and then to keep them honest. But that's not the point. The point is, can they feed everyone? Can they even feed themselves?'

'Are you all right? Do you need to take a break?'

'Don't change the subject.'

'Curtin says that these dizzy spells are becoming very dangerous. They're a sign that you're at Stage Three.'

'She hasn't said anything about stages to me. It's a new disease. If it's got stages, it's because she's making them up.'

'She doesn't want you knowing. She thinks it might hasten your deterioration.'

'But you know better than a doctor.'

'I know *you* better.'

'How many stages does she say there are?'

'Three.'

'Terrific.'

'And one of these days you're going to close your eyes and not wake up, and —'

'That's not relevant.'

'Not to you, maybe.'

'Anyway, I know my body. I've got plenty of fight left in me.'

'What if the situation — your health, I mean — becomes public knowledge?'

'Is that a threat?'

'Of course it's not. You know it's not. God! How can you even ask me that? Haven't I always been completely and utterly committed to what we set out to do? To what we achieved? Haven't I always played the team game? Haven't I always shown you the greatest respect? Haven't we danced this dance together for all these years? I'm not threatening you: I'm trying to help you, to save you.'

'Why does everybody want to save me?'

'Because you saved everybody.'

'*We* saved everybody … Oh, Christ, here it comes again.' He closed his eyes, fighting off a dizzy spell. 'I'm right about this. I'm —'

'Keep your eyes open,' Barton said. 'You make it worse when you close your eyes.'

'— I'm certain of it, I'm telling you: it's too soon.'

'No point just telling me. You have to convince me. I

can't take your word for it. Not this time.'

'Take my word for it? Nothing has changed. Nothing. Can we feed everyone with a few plants that may or may not be poisonous?'

'Today? No, of course not.'

'So, when? Tomorrow? The day after? Next week? Next decade? Next century? Never?'

'My projections say five years, if we get a wriggle on.'

'If if if.'

'That's near enough to tomorrow. There would need to be a transition period. Compassion at a local level, like it was when we started out, re-edits of file footage, supplemented by plants. But in time, plants will be the main supply, supplemented by compassion.'

'Five years! Those projections are a sham. Cleave will back me on this.'

'Come now. She doesn't play politics. She'd just "forget" to reply.'

'I'm telling you: sack your scientists. It'll take fifty years minimum. And even that's being wildly, crazily optimistic. And if we do it your way, we'll all die in the meantime.'

'Okay. If the dissenters must prove themselves — if they must fight to win, if they must prove that they can handle the consequences of winning — perhaps it's time we made it a fair fight.'

'Meaning what, exactly?'

'Fifty-fifty. You keep fighting them. I'll … give them a hand.'

'Hang on: "give them a hand". What do you mean by that? What do you actually mean? You mean "lead them", don't you? You mean "be them".'

Barton didn't reply. She just smiled a sad smile at Walker. She hadn't necessarily planned this break, this way, this day. She felt ripped open. But she knew — all of a sudden, she knew — that it was the right thing to do. The only thing. Listening to Walker flail around with arguments he knew weren't true clinched it for her. There was no way that Shine and Rise could carry on the way they were. But she also knew that Walker was right about one thing: they couldn't yet guarantee plants for everyone and they couldn't be certain whether there would be side effects. Even if they all just had new tumours, the strain on medical services would be overwhelming. What they needed was time.

'No, I won't do it. I don't want to fight you,' Walker said.

'We've always been at war.'

'But with a common purpose. This is different.'

'No, it's not. Our common purpose is unbroken. We'll be as united as we've ever been. United in war. Look, you can crush the resistance with a wave of your hand, without even leaving this room. You know you can.'

'Not without people knowing.'

'Sure, but just tell them they were extremists. Maniacs. Make something up.'

'I wouldn't need to make it up: they *are* terrorists.'

'They're not. You know they're not. But is that what you really want to do? Destroy them? If that's it, what's stopping you? Why haven't you done it already?'

Walker felt his heart start to race, his hands start to shake.

'Are you all right? Do you need me to call for help?' Barton asked.

'Shhhhh: I'm trying to think. I need to think.'

'But are you having a —'

'Fine. I'm fine, I tell you. I'm never f, f, fucking better. Just give me a minute.'

Walker sat with his eyes closed for so long that Barton could no longer tell if he was awake or asleep, alive or dead. When his hard, dry lips parted and he began a wretched snore, she stood, touching his cheek on her way out. She came away with powder on her fingers, and a smudge of blood.

As she reached the door, Walker called out. Somehow, through the fog of his mind, he was back with her. 'Let's talk tomorrow,' he said. 'You're bound to see things differently by then.'

Barton left the room without replying. After a moment, Hail and Curtin bustled in.

'Not now,' Walker muttered. 'Leave me be, I say. I'll call you when I'm ready.'

Hail was about to protest: he needed an update. Actually, given Walker's condition, he wished that he had been in the room for the leaders' meeting, not as a participant — he knew his place — but as an observer. He knew that Walker and Barton needed privacy. He knew that they fed off each other, that they had their own private rhythm. But these were not normal times: he had seen it in Barton's face. Change was afoot. Serious change. But Curtin held her hand up. They stood together, waiting, until Walker drifted back towards unconsciousness. Then Curtin unzipped his shirt, attached a new sensor, and retreated to the corner of the room. Hail eased into Barton's chair, to wait it out. To watch Walker sleep. But Walker sensed his presence.

'What. Is. It?' Walker asked, in between snores.

'I just wondered,' Hail said, 'if now was a good time to talk succession plans? Before it's too late.'

'Will you … serve Curtin?' Walker said.

'Yes, of course: with my entire being.'

Walker nodded and then nodded off. Hail glanced at Curtin. She was hunched over an autoscreen.

'Did you hear?' Hail whispered.

'Not now,' she said. 'I'm working.' A multi-screen of battle scenes appeared just beyond the tip of Walker's nose. 'Get ready to wake him up. He needs to see this. Now.'

'But did you hear what he said?'

'I heard. Shake him. Harder. Not that hard. Yes, good. Good.'

* * *

Sala slept late the next morning. She needed e-painkillers some nights, even though she'd healed — at least, as well as she would ever heal — weeks earlier. She was still lying on her bed, half-dozing, when the 'The Battle of Sergeant Sala' woke her. She threw a pillow at the autoscreen: it passed right through the footage of her crouching behind that ridiculous rock sitting in its splendid isolation. She let out a short, sharp scream of exasperation. Quickly, though, she fought for control over herself. She could not, would not, allow herself to wallow, to slip into dejection, rancour. Hold your head high, soldier, she told herself. Be proud, she told herself. If you must have fame, make the most of it, she told herself.

Wide awake and calm now, she spoke into her wearable. 'Turn off "The Battle of Sergeant Sala". Play "The Battle of Red Earth". No. Correction: play "The Aftermath of Year Seven". The highlights package.'

She fell back onto her bed. The autoscreen shifted, accommodating the fact that she was lying flat on her back. She watched the famous footage, still sharp, of ex-soldiers, their bodies damaged in some way or another, going about their days. She ate her fill of them, and then slept some more. She had nowhere she had to be, no one she wanted to see.

* * *

Malee sat in an interrogation room, on a straight-backed plastic chair. Two purple-clad military officers, a man and a woman, sat facing her. The interrogation had been going poorly, mainly, in Malee's view, because the officers assumed that she was lying to them when in fact she had nothing to hide. She was telling them the truth, at least so far as answering the questions they had the wit to ask. She certainly wasn't going to do their jobs for them. She was surprised to learn that they didn't have some device that they could point at her to make her reveal all.

'I'm terribly sorry to drag this out,' the man interrogator said, 'but I'm going to go ahead and ask you this one more time: who are you working with?'

'I told you already: I work alone.'

'Who supplied the seed that you used in your crime?' the woman interrogator asked.

'I took a train to District 35. But what crime?'

'Rough area,' the man interrogator said.

'Then I paid a woman to drive me further. I found the seed myself.'

'Who was this woman?' the woman interrogator asked. 'Name, address, known associates — if you'd be so kind.'

'I'd never met her before. I don't know her name. The vehicle was a Size One. That's all I can tell you, and I tell it to you happily. I could barely squeeze into it. But we didn't have to go far.'

'How much did you pay her?' the woman interrogator asked.

'One fifty.'

'Are you sure? Not to second-guess you, but only 150?' the man interrogator said.

'It was a lot of money to her. It's a lot to me.'

'I wouldn't go out there for 5,000,' the man interrogator said in a voice of wonder.

'Well, exactly,' the woman interrogator replied.

'Lady, could I politely suggest that it might be worth you reconsidering at least this part of your story?' the man interrogator said.

'Please don't call me "lady". My name is Malee.'

'Malee. Yes. Sorry. That was rude of me. It's nothing personal, but —'

'All right, let's not get bogged down debating your name,' the woman interrogator said. 'He apologises.'

'I really do,' the man interrogator said. 'It's just that I try to keep things nice and impersonal. It's how I was trained.'

'She probably doesn't need to know about our training.'

'It's not meant to be rude. It's meant to make things easier all round. Easier for us — it's a tough job we've got, as I'm sure you realise — and easier for you. If it's all right with you, I'll go ahead and think of you as a nameless citizen, for the purposes of this interview. That's a reasonable middle ground between "lady" and "Malee", I hope you'll agree.'

'Interrogation,' Malee said.

'I beg your pardon?'

'It's an interrogation, not an interview. And I'm a prisoner, not a citizen.'

'Now, *that's* rude,' the woman interrogator said.

'Yes, I'm a little hurt by your attitude, to be honest. A little insulted,' the man interrogator said. 'But I don't intend to stoop to your level. I learnt that in training too.'

'Fair enough,' Malee said, by now thoroughly bored.

'Who supplied the water?' the woman interrogator asked.

'I harvested it myself.'

'You ... *harvested* it? Harvested? But from where?'

'There are streams in the area where I found the seed —'

'"Streams"?' the woman interrogator said.

'She means water running along the ground, on top of the dirt,' the man interrogator said.

'I know what she means.'

'Please, don't snap at me.'

'I didn't.'

'You di—'

'That was the first time,' Malee cut across them. She was ready for this to be over — ready to be back in her cell. 'And the next time —'

'"The *next* time"?' the man interrogator said.

'That's what I said: the next time, I took it straight from the sky.'

'Not possible: the domefield goes up when there is a rain disturbance,' the woman interrogator said.

'Thanks be to Walker,' the man interrogator said.

'Thanks be to Walker,' the woman interrogator said, although Malee thought she used a desultory tone.

'You could say it too,' the man interrogator said to Malee, 'if you wanted to.'

'What?'

'You could say "Thanks be to Walker" too. It's no big deal. It's not a rule. Not a demand. It's just polite to say it when other people say it. My mum taught me that. Surely yours did too?'

'She didn't, funnily enough. But, sure, if it makes you happy. Thanks be to Walker. Thanks be to Barton. Thanks be to Ralphe. Thanks be to Spense. Thanks be to —'

'What about your mum?' the man interrogator said to the woman interrogator.

'All right, no need for an etiquette lesson,' the woman interrogator said.

'Yes, I'm getting off track, aren't I?'

'But do tell us,' the woman interrogator said, 'how did you harvest water from the sky?'

'When there are forecasts of a rain disturbance, I go outside the domefield area.'

'You've really got to work on your story, lady.'

'My name is Malee.'

'Don't let's start all that again,' the woman interrogator

said. 'Look, how about you tell us the names of your collaborators, and we can wrap things up here. We might even be able to let you out today. With your monitoring device left on, of course —'

'Of course,' Malee said.

'— and assuming you make certain undertakings to us.'

'We just want everyone to be happy,' the man interrogator added. 'Including you. Especially you.'

'I told you: I'm a movement of one. I've heard rumours that there are others like me. But I know nothing of these people. If you don't believe me, you might as well go ahead and torture me. Do your worst. I'm ready. I've already told you the truth, but it doesn't seem like it's the truth you're looking for.'

The woman interrogator was shocked. 'Torture you? We will do nothing of the sort. The very idea disgusts me.'

'A devastating suggestion,' the man interrogator said. He puffed himself up, and then deflated in his chair.

The woman interrogator gazed at him, half-sympathetic, half-exasperated. 'He's had a big week,' she said to Malee, 'and this just isn't helping.'

In that moment, Malee almost apologised. But she held her nerve and folded her arms, waiting for them to keep asking their questions.

* * *

'Aren't you hungry?' Walker said to Barton, inclining his head towards the autoscreen, on which 'The Battle of Sergeant Sala' silently played. 'I don't mind if you want to take a lunch break.'

Walker had slept tolerably well, and he was feeling as good as he'd felt in weeks. It didn't surprise him, this sudden rally. He'd long understood that he was at his best in a crisis. And it had been a long time since he'd had a proper one to deal with.

'I'm fine. I only left my rooms half an hour ago. But do you need a break?' Barton replied.

'Curtin will break us up when she thinks I need a rest. But I'm feeling great.'

'That's exactly what's got her worried.'

'But are you sure you're not hungry?'

'Nah, that's not my favourite battle.'

'I never did get your taste. That film is pure genius. It's the one bright spot in an average year.'

'I agree that it's technically superb. And Sergeant Sala herself does brilliant work. And the people love it. I can see why it's been so successful, but it's just not for me. To be honest, I think your people are running it a little too often.'

'You could always play something else. One of yours, maybe.'

'I told you, I'm fine: I ate earlier.'

Barton flashed a broad smile, and held her lips back, inviting Walker to lean in for a close look.

'What's that stuck between your teeth?' he asked.

Barton closed her mouth, sucked hard, and ran her tongue over her teeth. She opened her mouth.

'Better?'

'Now it's on the tip of your tongue.'

'I know.'

'What is it?' he asked again.

'Surely you remember spinach.' Barton touched her tongue with a fingertip and lifted the speck of green matter towards Walker. 'Want to touch it?' she asked.

'No thanks,' he said.

'You don't seem surprised.'

'I've been doing a lot of thinking since yesterday.'

'From what I heard, you were passed out most of the time.'

'Didn't stop me from thinking. Mostly about you.'

'Know your enemy, eh?'

He nodded. 'Know your enemy. But how long have you been … ?'

Walker found himself unable to finish his sentence. He wasn't shocked: he'd known something was afoot. But he didn't want to say the words.

'Eating plants? I try them now and again. I would never ask my people to do anything I wouldn't do myself. We've got a small research facility. That's all.'

'What does small mean?'

'A few thousand plants: thirty or so varieties. We need

to know what the dissenters know. We need to know more than they know.'

* * *

Geraldina was looking for her spare wearable — hers was playing up again: she really just needed to replace it — when she found Flake's photograph of the close-up of Sala hidden in the cupboard in the lounge room. She stared at it for a long moment. She knew exactly who it was. She knew what it was. She slipped it back where she had found it, behind the box that held Flake's family papers, or at least the few his mother had salvaged, from the Old Time. Geraldina herself had nothing from the Old Time, not even a photograph of her parents and her older sister, darling Misha, who was the first to go, her bathroom collapse a mystery but for the brown ooze draining from one ear.

'I'm just going out for a walk,' she called to Flake.

'Want me to come with you?' Flake replied from another room. 'The children are asleep. I could turn on the monitors in their rooms.'

'No, you stay here. I won't be long.'

'You okay?'

'Never better.'

* * *

Malee sat in her prison cell, making a show of staring at the wall. They'd allowed her a choice of 100 books, text or audio, but these were wholesome and affirming stories, the lot of them, and even a few paragraphs left her irritated and empty. She wanted them — Gaite, the interrogators, anyone else staring at her without giving her the chance to stare back — to witness her serenity. She was prepared to sit patiently in this cell for the rest of her life, thinking her reasonable thoughts, heading home only when the whole of Rise was eating plants and they had no memory of why they'd locked her up.

The voice of a guard boomed through the speakers: 'Time for dinner, girls and boys. Tuck in.'

Malee braced herself, but no screen appeared before her. She could hear the sounds of war coming from adjacent cells. She recognised 'The Battle of Jaeke and Gill', one of the great films of the war's classic middle period. Just hearing snippets of it was enough to fill her up. But she barely noticed that she was eating. Instead, she gazed into the gloomy emptiness of her cell, where her autoscreen should have been. Why were they withholding footage from her? She had no idea what it meant, and she tried not to jump to conclusions. But she was alive with hope. And fear. And suspicion.

* * *

Wedge's task was to camp out in the abandoned buildings amongst the drifters of District 87, near the entrance to Holland's plant room, and to keep tabs on who came and went, to look for patterns, clues, hints. He thought he could have been doing something more useful. These were momentous times, after all. But he believed in following orders, and in playing his part, for the greater good. So he sat around, watching and waiting while nothing happened.

***

It was time. Dinn and the rest of her group of dissidents, a couple of vehicle-loads of strangers who had found each other and who made it their business not to ask each other too many questions, drove past a sign that read 'National Concert Hall'. The plants they carried with them came from their pooled efforts, but, to her shame, Dinn's ear of corn hadn't received clearance in time. She was certain, because she just knew, that the crop was safe. But she agreed that they couldn't risk it. If they poisoned people, they'd lose the struggle before they even started. But, still, she felt like an intruder, turning up empty-handed.

The place seemed deserted, like so many of the remaining landmark buildings from the Old Time. Dinn and the others parked the vehicles in a service lane, put soft masks over their faces, and slipped into the property over the low fence at the back. In their packs, they had corn, green-grey zucchinis, a few hard baby tomatoes. It was a meagre offering, but they knew, because they had a supporter inside the National Concert Hall who had painted a dire picture, that people were dying. They had to do whatever they could whenever they could. And they weren't sure how long the plants would last before they rotted. What a thing, Dinn thought, to be pitching perishables against war footage, which lasted forever.

Dinn led the way through the door their supporter had promised would be unlocked. She worried about the others. She'd seen fear and uncertainty in the faces of a couple of them before they'd put on their masks. But she barely knew these people. She didn't know how to give them the resolve they needed. Neither did she know how to casually tell them that she was Commander Holland's beloved sister. 'Courage, friends,' she whispered. How lame, she thought, but they all murmured 'courage' back to her.

She led the group silently and swiftly through dim corridors and up a staircase. They avoided the floor–ceiling elevators as a precaution, although they had the codes. It only took them a couple of minutes to reach the vast angled hall where the patients lay. With nervous nods of solidarity, but no words, they fanned out. Dinn counted heads. There were still seven of them. No one had got lost. No one had fled. Hardly an army.

As Dinn gently shook her first patient, she was shocked, even though she'd known exactly what to expect, to see his belly rising from beneath the sheet. And he smelt like an Old Time type of putrid. She shook him again, harder.

'No. What?' the man said. He lifted his bald head up, confused. Dinn saw that the last of his hair stayed on the pillow.

'Shhhhh,' Dinn said. 'I'm here to help you.'

'Thank you, thank you, you're all very nice to help me.'

'Open your mouth.'

'Yes, all right. Why?'

Dinn dropped a piece of zucchini into the man's mouth. 'Chew. Swallow,' she said.

'Chew? What? Chew, what do you mean, chew?'

'Shhhhh, please. Use your jaw to make your teeth move around in your mouth. Then swallow what's in your mouth.'

'What is in my mouth?'

'It doesn't matter what it is.'

'How did it get there?'

'Let it go all the way down your throat. And don't speak again. And don't talk about this later.'

'But I don't underst—'

'Hold still,' Dinn said. She held the man still with one hand on his shoulder, causing him to cry out. With her other hand, she closed his mouth and stroked his throat, forcing a swallow. 'Sorry,' she whispered before moving on to the next patient.

Lying awake in another section of the vast room,

Grainy sensed movement. But there was no moving autotorch, the usual sign that a nurse or doctor was responding to an emergency. Then he heard whispering. He pushed his wasted torso up for a better view, putting immense pressure on his elbows. Even though the doctors had put him on a concentrated diet of twice-hourly battle footage, excessive for a healthy person, he had deteriorated since they'd admitted him. The doctors had told him they didn't know what was wrong with him. Grainy trusted them, even though it was obvious to him that everyone in the room had the same illness as he did. He always remembered to thank them for their candour and for their efforts, but he wondered if they knew something they weren't telling him. And he didn't understand why he couldn't call his daughter, just to say hello.

As Grainy's eyes adjusted to the gloom, he saw a shadowy figure moving about, stooping down, offering a few quiet words to a patient, giving them something. In another part of the room, he saw another figure doing the same thing. And another.

A door close to Grainy opened, near what had once been the concert stage. A squad of military police entered. They moved swiftly and with no attempt at stealth, their goggles breaking through the dark. Grainy stayed sitting up, although he sensed it would be safer for him if the police didn't see him watching. His shoulder roared with pain now, but he wanted to see, even though he had no idea what he was seeing.

The military police paired off and quickly arrested the intruders. There was no violence, no aggro, not even any raised voices, although it seemed to Grainy that urgent whispers echoed off the walls and the ceiling. Words came to him in strange patterns, leaving him even more confused. He wondered if he was hallucinating.

Now in groups of three, the police and the shadowy figures moved quietly and in an unfussed fashion towards the exit. As one group passed close by, Grainy saw that the person the police were escorting wore a cloth mask.

Dinn wasn't overly surprised when a military police officer took her arm and whispered, 'Time to go, if you would be so kind.' She had worried — they all had — that it'd been too easy to find the location of the hospital, or prison, or illness farm, or whatever it was. As a group, they'd acknowledged the dangers but resolved that they had no choice but to deliver their plants while they were edible.

'Lead the way,' she whispered to the officer.

A second officer eased the pack off Dinn's back, but neither officer checked her closed hand. As the three of them moved along the row, past fitful and comatose patients, Dinn flicked a piece of zucchini into the air. It landed on Grainy's distended stomach and bounced onto his bed. He reached out, found the object in the creased sheet, and squeezed the strange substance — not hard, not soft — between two shaking fingers. It felt disgusting.

Alive, somehow. With what little strength he had, he flung the object as far away as he could, and sunk back into the bed with a groan.

***

Late that same night, Sala sat in the Grand Lake Bar, idly watching 'The Battle of Dusty Plain'. It had always been one of her favourites. Her old friend Tressle, who she'd drifted apart from, had lost both of her kneecaps that day. Sala didn't want to be one of those ex-soldiers who ate so little that they made themselves sick. She watched Tressle rolling about in the dirt. She watched herself calm Tressle and help carry her to safety. She missed Tressle. She had no desire to ever see her again.

It occurred to her that they could have called every single film ever made 'The Battle of Dusty Plain'. Apart from the camaraderie with the other fighters, apart from the adrenaline rushes, it was the dust that she missed most of all. The feel of it on her, on her face, the way it got inside her uniform and patterned her body. These days, she was always clean and fresh. She found it dislocating. Distasteful, even.

She wondered why Commander Holland had asked to see her. It was odd. But she couldn't turn him down, even if he was now her ex-boss. She supposed he wanted to commiserate, to check on her welfare, to tick that empathy box. Or maybe he had some off-site consultancy work to offer her. She hoped he wasn't after anything more: she didn't think Holland was *that* sort of boss, but the soldiers had always gossiped about him because he had no visible private life, no apparent secret weekend world. And, she thought, people in power misuse their power in the end, one way or another, don't they?

She'd insisted to Holland that they meet at the Grand Lake Bar. She was pretty sure he would hate the place, which suited her just fine. She was watching Tressle writhe around on the screen, wondering how she was doing, wondering if she was happy, wondering how the knee replacements had taken, wondering if she'd adjusted well or poorly to post-war life, wondering how she managed pain, managed memories, when Holland pushed open the door. He flicked his wearable at the entry point, lifted the hood off his grey, thinning hair, and absorbed the shock of the patrons who recognised him.

Sala saw Holland's reflection in the bar mirror but didn't react. He was well-preserved, she thought, given what his body had endured at the end of the Old Time. She watched him look around, locate the back of her head, and start to move towards her. His face was blank. Unreadable. Decades of training, she supposed.

As he reached her table, Sala rose.

'Sergeant Sala reporting for duty, sir.'

'At ease, Sala, for Chrissakes.'

'Yes, SIR.'

Holland peered at her, unsure if she was angry or nervous or merely amusing herself.

'It's good to see you … Hell, I mean … sorry,' he said.

'Don't fuss. These days, no one can even look at me without fucking it up,' Sala said.

'That's exactly why I'm sorry. And I'm sorry that it's come to this.'

'Sorry this, sorry that. Well, discharge from the army was inevitable, that's what they told me when I was inducted. You probably told me yourself.'

'And it's true. And I stand by it. But you were one of the best. Most of them — they were good, don't get me wrong, I've got no complaints — but most of them were just passing through. Good but not great. You were different. You were special.'

Something about the way he said 'special' pricked Sala. 'Have you called me here to hit on me, sir?' she said, in a bored tone. 'Because, look —'

'No, my God, not at all, I —'

'— because I'm awfully bored of men and their hot and heavy dreams and schemes.'

'You've got me all wrong. I wouldn't dream of doing anything to you —'

'*With* me. Jesus Fucking Christ in a helmet. *With* me.'

'Yes, indeed, I, with you, but that's not, I still wouldn't, it would be entirely inappropriate and I just wouldn't, not that you wouldn't deserve the attention, no, what I mean to say is, that's not what I'm here for … Look, I'm sorry. I know living a normal life isn't your thing, believe me, I know —'

'Define "normal".'

'Yes. Quite right. I mean civilian life. But you couldn't have stayed in the field. You just couldn't. Not after that.' He pointed at her face. 'You must know that.'

'What are you doing here, sir?'

'I'm on peace-conference leave.'

'That's not what I meant.'

'Yes, I know. I asked to meet you because —'

He stopped speaking as Sala's face appeared on the screen. 'Oh, for the love of God,' he said.

As the patrons in the bar cheered and clapped, Sala stood and bowed extravagantly.

Holland stood too. 'Appalling behaviour, all of you,' he told the room, swinging about, including everyone in his censure. 'Have some respect. Have some decency.'

'Have a little tenderness,' someone called out.

'Who said that?' Holland demanded to know. 'I'll have you know that this soldier —'

'I can look after myself, thanks, Dad,' Sala said mildly.

'I've got a good mind to —'

'Stop it,' Sala said. 'I'm a regular here. These people are my friends.' She peered at one bloke who was openly leering at her. 'Well, most of them, most of the time. Hey,

Tone, I think you've had more than enough warfare for one day. Go home and sleep it off, eh? And you,' she said to Holland, 'for Chrissakes, sit down and shut up.'

As Holland sat, he gave the man called Tone a final piercing glare.

'Look, we shouldn't stay here much longer,' Holland told Sala. 'So, listen —'

'Yes, SIR. I'm listening, SIR.'

'Please. I asked you to meet me because I trust you. Because I think you know the score.'

'The score?'

'Because I have a sense that you might be willing to believe some of the things that I have come to believe. Especially now. After ... your injuries, I mean. But even before that. Maybe. Perhaps. At least in part. A start. An inkling. I hope.'

'I haven't got a fucking clue what you're talking about, sir.'

'Deep down, I think you do.'

'I really don't. Are you unwell? Is there someone I can call for you? What about your bigwig doctor friend? Curtin, is it? Or Walker's lackey. Hick, right? Hacked?'

'You know his name. And he deserves your respect.'

'Or the big man himself. If you're not feeling yourself, surely Walker needs to know.'

'I'm in the best shape I've been in for years. Maybe forever.'

'Mind you, Walker is hardly looking on top of the world himself, if you want my opinion.'

'Please. Listen. I'm trying to share a secret with you. A big secret. A life-changing, life-giving secret.'

'But why me?'

'Because I've watched you closely from your first day of training.'

'Monitored me, you mean?'

'Yes: that's exactly what I mean. And your tests have always been fine — nothing exceptional, but fine —'

'Gosh, thanks.'

'Which is why I've never put too much stock in tests. Because you've always operated on some higher level.'

'No, I haven't. I just happen to be your most recent casualty. The most recent one you didn't accidentally kill, at least.'

'No, I've commanded hundreds of soldiers, and here I am, choosing to talk to you.'

'Just how closely have you been monitoring me?'

'I'm sorry, that's classified information.' He leant in close. 'Things are changing. And they must change more. There are only a few of us, so far. But we will grow in numbers. We need a civilian leader.'

'I have no idea what you're talking about.'

'I know you don't. And I can't explain it. Not here. But I can show you.'

Holland got off his stool and tugged at Sala's elbow.

'Get off me.'

'Please, you need to come with me.'

'I really don't.'

'It's the only way. You won't regret it.'

'Yeah, I've heard that line plenty of times.'

'Shhh. Don't make a scene.'

'A scene? *A scene?* Fuck y—'

'I want to show you something astonishing —'

'Here we go. I suppose it's big and hard, this astonishing "something" you've got to show me. I warned you that if you hit on me, I'd —'

'No no no, I told you, it's nothing like that. Listen, this is the most important thing you'll ever see. It'll change everything. For all of us. Everything.'

Something in his desperate tone finally registered with Sala. She stared at him hard. Here was an unflappable man, a leader who wore a mask in public, ripping himself to shreds and floating in the breeze, all in the hope that she might hear him.

'Okay,' she said. 'Let's go.'

Holland stood in the doorway of the bar for only a few seconds before he pulled the hood over his head. But in those few seconds, a street camera captured his face, identified him, and transported the footage to Bull and Boosie.

'Hoo-hah, we've located him,' Boosie said. 'He's on the move. And he's got a lady with him, lucky bastard. We're definitely going to need drones for this little rendezvous.'

'Hang on, that's not a lady … isn't that … Oh Lord in Heaven Who I Don't Believe In,' Bull said. 'We've got a … a …'

'What we've got is a fucking diplomatic incident,' Boosie said. 'Or maybe it's the romance of the century. Either way, we're watching history unfold.' He turned to Bull. 'What fun, hey? What fun!'

***

Many districts away, Wedge sat in an abandoned building, half-watching 'The Battle of Foot Wounds' while he loaded and unloaded and loaded and unloaded his stun gun. He pointed it at himself, but then thought, 'What's the point?'

***

'Don't walk with me,' Holland told Sala. He was in battle mode now. 'Count to fifteen before you move. Don't look at me directly. After fifty metres, I'll stop and look in a window of a hat shop. Walk straight past me. Don't stop. Don't speak to me. Don't acknowledge me in any way. After you pass me, take the second right. It's an unnamed alley. Walk 100 metres. When you reach a door with a red handle, wait for me.'

'Can I step on the cracks on the sidewalk?' Sala asked.

'Please, no speaking. Not until I give you the all clear.'

'No stepping on the cracks. No stepping on the crackpots.'

'Sergeant. Please.'

'Ex-Sergeant, if you don't mind.'

'Just don't talk to me or look at me until I tell you it's safe. Okay?'

'You're the boss. Or you were.'

Holland kept his expression utterly blank, his eyes directed at his feet, as he began walking. Sala counted to fifteen in her head, and then sauntered off, struggling to wipe the amused expression from her face. When she passed Holland gazing at the hat display — all of them the same shade and colour, so far as Sala could tell — she reached out and pinched his bottom.

'Oh my,' she murmured. 'Such firm Old Time flesh.'

* * *

'Did she just do what I think she did?' Boosie yelled. 'Oh me, oh my, she just fucking groped him, get me stills, get me close-ups, get me the whole thing on a loop, what a moment, what a coup.'

* * *

As Sala continued walking, she noticed a camera on the wall of a building opposite. There were cameras everywhere these days, although usually you had to look hard to find them. Sala wasn't too fussed. It reminded her of the constant scrutiny of fighting in the war, and she'd given up any pretence of the right to privacy the day she'd signed up. But she didn't like the one-sidedness of it. If Walker's purple people wanted to look at her, fair enough: Christ knows she had nothing to hide. And Christ knows that she had nothing much else to do. But she would have liked some reciprocity: why couldn't she see the face, the name, the life history, the grief levels of the person watching her? She gave the camera a slow wink and kept on her way.

* * *

'Oh my God, she winked at me,' Bull said. 'Right at me. Did you see?'

'At you? Dream on, buster,' Boosie said. 'It's me she wants. Only me.'

'Stuff what she wants: she's all I've ever wanted. That should be enough. Devotion is contagious, isn't it?'

'You're disgusting, buddy.'

'What do you mean?'

'What you call devotion, I call stalking. Bull the Bully.'

'Hey, it's my job to observe,' Bull said. 'And I don't

really mean it. I'm just playing around. But maybe she's sending us a message. Maybe he's taken her hostage.'

'Okay, come on, concentrate: let's not lose Commander Traiterman again,' Boosie said.

'Do you think they're … you know … together?'

'Will you shut up? Let's split the screens. We need to watch them both. I'll watch Sala, you watch Holland.'

'Why do you get to watch Sala?' Bull complained.

'Because you're overheated, buster. Look at them: it's like they've gone their separate ways, but they're still connected somehow, by an invisible rope. What do you think? Is she in on it? Growing the plants?'

'It's not my job to speculate. It's disrespectful to Sala and her legacy,' Bull said.

'Maybe she's bitter. You know, about her face.'

'And *you're* calling *me* overheated.'

'Don't pout. Just have a guess: is she guilty or not guilty?' Boosie asked.

'Wait and see. That's the job: look, listen, smell. And don't speculate.'

'Dammit, I know what the job is. I'm just asking you your opinion. For the fun of it. You know, fun? Hahahahaha, fun? The joy of life?'

'All right: if it'll shut you up, she's innocent. Of course she is.'

'How can you say that?'

'You asked for my opinion,' Bull said. 'That's my opinion.'

'But that's because you want to f—'

'Look at her: she's got no idea what he's up to. She's got no idea where they're going.'

'What happened to not guessing?' Boosie asked.

'I'm *not* guessing. I'm analysing the evidence.'

'No way. You're so wrong. Look at the way they're weaving in and out, magically missing each other. That's expert choreography.'

'If you don't want me to guess, don't ask me to guess,' Bull said. 'Look, we should call this in, eh?'

'What's the rush? Let it play out. Let's see what they get up to with each other. Because if the good commander hits the jackpot — if you take my meaning — it's our duty to be there for the whole event.'

'We can't wait: she's a Code One.'

'What? No, I don't think so.'

'It said so in yesterday's Daily Report.'

'Oh, I … I never read that thing.'

'I know you don't,' Bull said. 'And so does Annar.'

'But Code One? Why Sala? It doesn't make sense.'

'It's not our job to know why. It's our job to watch who we're told to watch, and to report when we're told to report.'

'But a Code One? Just because of that face? A bit of mangled skin?'

'You're disgusting.'

Boosie banged the table. '*I'm* disgusting? You're the one with a scar fetish.'

'It's not a fetish. Don't call it that.' Bull began to whimper.

'Oh, shit,' Boosie said. 'Not again. I'm sorry, buddy. But please: don't start all that again. I was just playing around with you. Just teasing.'

Boosie patted Bull on the back, but it was too late.

'I'm so lonely,' Bull wailed. 'And you push. Every time, you push and push.'

'I'm sorry that you think that. But, come on, get a grip now: we're working. We've got a Code One.'

'I know.'

'You're being so so so unprofessional.'

'I know … but don't judge me,' Bull said. He dropped his head. 'It's just that when I watch Sala getting shot like that, I don't know if it's her, if it's really her pain that gets to me, or someone else's pain, or if it's just that I've got nobody in my life.'

'Hey, you've got me,' Boosie said. 'But only if you get it together.'

'I've bought "The Battle of Sergeant Sala" and —'

'Everyone's bought it. Relax: that's normal.'

'— and it's the best battle I've ever seen, and I love her, but I can't really love her, can I, because I've never even met her, but she does stand for something, doesn't she, or someone? But how do I go and find this someone else if I don't know who that someone else is?'

'You eat too much. It's not healthy.'

'I know.'

'Maybe you need a stint in rehab.'

'No, they'll give me the sack. I can sort it out myself.' Bull sat up, flicked his hair out of his eyes, and spoke into his wearable. 'Find Annar … Hey, boss. Yeah, sorry, I know it's late, but I've got some footage.'

'*We've* got some footage,' Boosie yelled. 'We're a fucking team, aren't we?'

'Yeah, me and Boosie have got some footage for the bigwigs. The situation is still in progress. I'm sending through what we've got now. It's a Code One.'

***

Holland found Sala leaning against the door with the red handle.

'Let's go. Quick,' he said. He touched the door open, beckoned her to go inside, and pulled the door shut behind them. They walked through a dusty house, sparsely furnished.

'Where are we?' Sala asked.

'Nowhere yet,' Holland said.

'Does someone live here? Are we breaking in?'

'No. But that's not important. Come on, keep up.'

Holland led Sala to a room filled with skeletal chairs. He dragged a haphazardly stacked pile of them from one corner, revealing a trapdoor — not a ceiling–floor lift but an actual Old Time door in the floor. He pulled a handle, and the door opened upwards.

'Nifty,' Sala said.

'You go first,' Holland said. 'You'll need to turn your autotorch on.'

'I'd have worn my uniform if I'd known we were going on a field trip. Except I can't get the bloodstains out of it.'

Sala stepped onto a vertical ladder. Holland followed. At its bottom, they were in a tunnel, just tall enough for them to walk upright.

'This way,' Holland said. 'Watch out: the roof is low.'

'Yes, I can see that.'

They walked for ten minutes in the dark, led by their autotorches, until the tunnel opened up into a bigger space.

'The old train lines,' Holland said. 'They run all over the place, under the city.'

'But no train for us, eh?'

'There's no need,' Holland said, delighted with himself. 'May I present you with your ride?' Before them stood a decommissioned military vehicle.

'That old heap?' Sala said. But she got in. 'I'll drive, shall I?' she said.

* * *

'Park over there,' Holland said. 'We go on foot from here. It's not far.'

'Finally,' Sala said. 'Where the hell are we?'

'I can't tell you, exactly. Not yet. Not until you've committed.'

'Committed to what?'

'You'll see. Please: have a little patience. It'll be worth it. I promise.'

'So many promises. I might just head back home. Can I borrow your wheels?'

'Sergeant Sala. Stand to attention! Now!'

'You're the one who keeps telling me that I'm delisted.'

'That's exactly why we're here. We need people of your calibre for a new struggle. Your experience. Your courage. I hope you'll join us. I believe you are destined for greatness.'

'"We"? Who's "we"? What struggle?'

'You'll see. Have —'

'A little fucking patience, blah blah blah.'

'Exactly.'

She lifted her head to the roof of the tunnel they now walked through. 'Try a little patience,' she sang, while Holland did his best to pretend it wasn't happening, 'try a little hope, try a little light relief, try a little belief, try a little longing, try a little tenderness.'

'Okay, this is it,' he said, pained. 'We're here. Up this ladder.'

They climbed into an empty room.

'Not a word, if you please,' Holland said. 'And stay low.'

They skirted the perimeter of the room. Holland stood in front of a wall and placed his hand on the soiled paint. The wall slid open and they stepped into the room of plants.

Holland hung back, while Sala stalked about the room, dirt on the soles of her shoes.

'Well, fuck me,' she said eventually.

'Well? What do you think?'

'Are you kidding? How could you bring me here to see this?' She shoved him hard, and then again. 'Five deaths in a month: Benson, Ledbetter, Swift —'

'Stop. Please don't say their names. I can't bear it.'

'Benson. Ledbetter. Swift. Puru. Smiffee. Suddenly, it's all making perfect sense. You're a dirty fucking traitor. Swift, for fuck's sake — he worshipped you.'

'Now hang on. You've got it all wrong. I'm a man of honour. I would never put any of my people in that sort of danger deliberately. How could you even —'

'"My people",' Sala said. 'There's no way you get to call them "my people". Not now. Not in this room, this —'

'Each incident was unrelated to the —'

'Each incident? Don't you mean each DEATH?'

'Yes. That's what I mean. Each death. And each death was either natural causes or an accident. Truly. You have to believe me. I mean, you were there when Smiffee did those push-ups, weren't you? He did it to himself.'

'How can you even —'

'None of the deaths have anything to do with … with … all this. People die in wars. Accidents happen. I would never —'

'Hero to the people by day, fair-minded dissident by night. That's literally unbelievable. Where's your loyalty? Did you eat it?'

Holland reached the limit of his reserves of patience. 'How dare you lecture me about loyalty?' he snapped. 'I've given everything and more to this city.' He caught himself, paused, and tried again: 'Look, I understand why you're upset, but —'

'Oh, thank you very much for understanding, you traitor, you bastard, you —'

'— but this is something new. Something alive. Something fresh. And yet something old. Something regained. Something polished. This is for the future. Just take a look: this is for you.'

'For me?' Sala whispered, her fury too much to raise her voice. 'For me?'

'For you. And for everyone who has fought the war. It's your vindication.'

'And what about this?' She pointed at her face, grabbing the scarring and pulling on it. 'What's this for? Who is vindicated by my scars?'

'That's … that's … for … the people too. All the people. And they're immeasurably grateful. As they should be. You've filled them up. But not all of them.

Because nothing stays the same.'

She advanced on him and tried to rub the damaged side of her face against his face.

'Stop it,' he said. 'Please don't.'

She pushed him to the ground, straddled him, and continued rubbing her face in his face.

'What am I supposed to do now?' she yelled. 'What *am* I now? Should I go to the museum, let them stuff me and shove me behind glass: "Once upon a time, she sacrificed the rest of her life" — and the people said, "Thanks, love" and "Top effort" and "Pass the potatoes, would you, sweetheart?"'

'I'm sorry, so so sorry, about your face. But it's not as if you're dead. It's —'

'I don't give a shit about my face. You took my war away.'

'No. It was a bullet from the enemy. That's war. That's why you were there. You know this. We always had such high hopes for you. It was clear from early on that you were elite. But, still, we never expected a moment so … perfect.'

'You orchestrated it.'

'No.' Holland pushed her off him and got to his feet.

Sala came at him again. 'You deserve to get a piece of it,' she said. 'Come on. Suck my face. Don't you want to know what my scar tissue tastes like?'

'No, I told you, I don't want … that.'

Sala threw a switchblade at his feet. 'Better still, why don't you have a go at the other side? Even things up.' She offered him her unblemished cheek. 'What's the matter with you? Got nobody to do your dirty work for you? Here, let me help.' She picked up the knife and flicked the blade open and turned it on herself. 'What do you think, a symmetrical pattern? Or random slashes? Surface or deep? Should I take out an eye, maybe?'

Holland, who prided himself on his ability to read people, had no idea if Sala was truly enraged or if she was toying with him. Deciding not to risk it, he grabbed Sala's wrist and held it tight until she dropped the knife. He pushed her, hard, towards the plants. She fell over.

'All right,' Sala said. 'No need to beat me up. I was just making a point.'

Holland picked up the knife and pocketed it, just to be sure.

'You're a coward,' Sala said. 'And a traitor.'

'No: I'm for survival. You'd be surprised who's starving. And it'll only get worse.'

'This — all of this — wouldn't feed you and me for a week.'

'This is just the beginning. Believe me.'

Sala walked amongst the plants. She reached out towards a half-ripe tomato but checked herself.

'Go on. Touch it.'

'No. No, I won't.' But despite her anger, she felt the

wonder of new life around her. 'I, I never thought I'd … is that an orange?'

'Capsicum.'

Sala crouched down and sniffed the capsicum. 'Impossible,' she said.

'It's yours, if you want it, when it's ripe.'

'God, no.'

'It's perfectly safe.'

'I'll never be that hungry.'

A beeping noise interrupted them. A pipe groaned, and a moment later a row of sprinklers began to send a faint spray of water over the plants. Sala screamed and ran out of the water, pulling her clothes off, rolling in dry dirt. Holland laughed and stepped under the water. He opened his mouth and drank the mist. He danced around the plants, mouth agape, while Sala, in her underwear, picked up clumps of dirt and scrubbed herself raw.

* * *

Boosie cheered and Bull watched rapt as Sala stripped and rolled in the dirt. They switched cameras repeatedly, trying to find the best angles. Above the plant room, Wedge sat and waited for something to happen, oblivious to the action he was missing. And in Walker Compound, Walker, Curtin, and Hail watched the feed live.

'So much water,' Walker murmured to himself in

wonder. 'Oh, Willy, what are you thinking?'

'I'm sorry, boss,' Hail said. 'I was worried about him, but I had no idea it was this serious. Look at him: he's standing in it. Just letting it fall on him. He's drinking it, for Chrissakes.'

'It must be safe,' Curtin said. 'It can't be, but it must be.'

'Cleave already has a water sample,' Walker said.

'Don't tell me: you're having trouble getting her to prioritise it.' Hail gazed at the screen. 'He's lost his mind. It's devastating.'

'Don't fret. It's for the best,' Walker said.

'But it's Holland. He's betrayed you. He's betrayed everything we fought for.'

'Still, it's nice to see he's still got some fight in him, some life, don't you think? I was getting worried about him.'

'Nice?'

'Nice,' Walker confirmed. 'We don't want him clapped out before he starts his new assignment.'

'He's standing in a room full of plants, getting wet, and you're talking nice? … What new assignment?' Hail asked.

'Okay, I've seen enough for now,' Walker said.

'I haven't,' Curtin said. She turned on her personal autoscreen. 'Play it again,' she murmured. 'Fast-forward … stop.' She watched water hitting human skin, fascinated.

'What do you think?' Walker asked her.

'It's a tiny operation,' Curtin said. 'But we can assume

it's a model. A dry run, as it were. We can assume that he's turned, and turned for good.'

'He's lost his mind,' Hail said.

'He hasn't,' Curtin said. 'He's changed his mind. But he's still our Holland.'

'Okay,' Walker said. 'We'd better arrest him. Tonight. But tell them to wait until he's alone. I've got to go.'

'Go? Go where? Do you need me?' Hail said.

'No. We're going to need to extend the peace talks. Can you deal with that?' Walker said to Hail.

'Of course. But why?'

'Barton and I need some more time. There have been some developments. I have work to do. I'll need you for a few hours,' he told Curtin. 'And I need the latest data and analysis on the illness. Everything you've got. And I need you to keep me awake.'

'You need me to keep you alive,' Curtin said.

'Yeah, that too.'

'And you need me to walk you wherever you're going.'

'Yeah, that too.'

'But these developments,' Hail said. 'Are they good developments or bad developments?'

'Let's just say, we may need the presidents to share some news with the people.'

'News news or real news?' Hail said.

'Keep them talking for at least another day. Maybe two.'

'Our Mr President may need a sweetener. He's already bored out of his mind.'

'Tell him he's about to get all the action he could possibly ask for.'

* * *

The next morning, Flake and Geraldina sat up in bed, the children at their feet.

'Time to get ready for school, you two,' Flake said.

'Can you help me?' the girl asked.

'Me too?' the boy asked.

'You get started. I'll be in soon.'

He waited for them to leave the room. Then he turned to Geraldina. 'I've got something to show … what I mean is … I've got something to tell you. Something important.'

'Okay.'

'I … well, I need to show you something, really. Can you wait here?'

'Sure, love.'

Flake plodded into the lounge room and retrieved the plain envelope from its hiding place. Geraldina sat unmoving, waiting, listening to the kids bicker about who owned a shirt they both wanted to wear.

'It fits me.'

'No, it fits me.'

'It suits my complexion.'

'No, it suits my complexion.'

Flake sat on the edge of the bed and handed Geraldina the envelope.

'Open it,' he said.

She slipped her hand into the envelope and pulled out the photograph of Sala's skin. She looked at it, nodding.

'It's Sergeant Sala,' he said.

'I know.'

'It's her cheek. Close-up.'

'I know what it is.'

'I'm so ashamed. I'm so sorry. Can you ever forgive me? I just … I just wanted, needed, the detail. I don't know why. I needed to hold it. I couldn't help myself. I can't explain it. But I felt like there was something missing, something I needed, something this could fix. But it's not about you. It's truly not.'

Geraldina patted his arm and climbed out of bed.

'What are you doing? Where are you going?' Flake said.

'Wait here.'

'Please, please don't leave me,' he pleaded. 'Let's talk this through. I'll do anything you ask. It'll never happen again. I swear. It's like a disease, like a —'

'I said, wait there. I'll just be a second.'

Flake nodded, defeated. While he waited, he gazed at the photo. He knew he was doing the right thing, telling her, giving the image up. But he was going to miss it. He was still jumping between guilt about owning the photo to mourning its loss when Geraldina walked back in and handed him an envelope.

'Have a look,' she said.

Flake opened the envelope and pulled out a photograph. He gazed from his photo to Geraldina's photo and back again: they were an exact match. He lifted his eyes and met Geraldina's steady gaze.

'From what I hear,' Geraldina said, 'half the city has gone out and bought one.'

'But … it's wrong. It's still wrong,' Flake said. 'Isn't it?'

'Terribly wrong,' Geraldina said.

'But you don't seem too fussed about it. I lie awake at night worrying. What does it mean? Why do I need it? … Why do you need it?'

'Is it the worst thing we'll ever do in our lives?'

'It's so disrespectful to her … to Sala, I mean. Such an invasion. And it's disrespectful to Walker, after all he's done for us. To Barton. To Mum and Dad, to your mum and dad, to Ruth and Ahmed, to Jill and Cassie —'

'Yes,' Geraldina said. 'Yes, it is. But we've got to live, best we can.'

'Who's helping me?' the little boy cried out, a room away.

'No, who's helping me?' the little girl yelled.

'No, me,' the boy said.

'No, me,' the girl said.

'No, me,' Flake murmured.
'No, me,' Geraldina said.

* * *

While Flake was walking the children to school, before heading to the office to work on the ever-vexing question of peace in the Old Time nation of Ethiopia, 1990–92, and while Geraldina logged on to work from home, her focus the gratuitous repeat bombing of the Old Time city of Hiroshima, Curtin walked Walker slowly into the meeting room at Walker Compound.

'Easy now,' Curtin said, helping him into a chair. Hail slipped in behind them, near the door, hoping he might be able to stay for the talks.

'You truly look like death,' Barton told Walker. 'But, hey, welcome to a new era.'

'What new era?' Hail said.

'Thirty minutes on, thirty minutes off,' Curtin said to Walker, 'or I'll cancel the whole day. I mean it.'

'Sorry I'm late,' Walker said to Barton. 'I had a busy night. Late night. Momentous night.'

'Thirty minutes,' Curtin said again. 'I mean it.'

'I've got people out finding you something new to eat,' Hail said to Walker. 'We'll bring it to you as soon as we can.'

'Good. But no more dogs. That ship has sailed.'

'All your ships have sailed,' Curtin murmured.

'Have a little faith,' Hail said. 'I put a lot of thought into your meals.'

'It's true,' Curtin said. 'It's all he thinks about these days.' She shone a light into Walker's eyes. 'Hmhhhff,' she muttered.

'You can leave now,' Walker said.

'I'll be right outside,' Curtin said.

'There's really no need.'

'Remember: thirty minutes on, thirty off,' she called, and the door closed behind her.

'You too, Hail,' Walker said.

'Don't worry,' Barton said, when she saw the look of disappointment on Hail's face. 'You'll be the first to hear of any final decisions.'

'Final decisions about what?' Hail said.

'We promise. Don't we, Walker?'

'We do,' Walker said.

Barton waited for Hail to leave — the doors seemed to take an age to open and close, as if Hail were willing them to stay open — before she finally spoke.

'You've told Curtin, then?' she said.

'Told her what?'

'And you've told Hail too.'

'Told them what?'

'That Curtin is your successor.'

'It's not for me to make such a decision. It's their decision.'

'Don't be silly. It's your call. Don't pretend otherwise. And I think you've already done it. They both know.'

'I'm … I don't think I did. Maybe I did.'

'Curtin should be in here now.'

'I'm not dead yet,' he said. 'But listen: I've got a present for you.' He spoke into his wearable. 'Please run the Code One footage from last night.'

An autoscreen appeared. After a moment, footage of Holland and Sala on their way to the plant room appeared.

'Oh my. You've been watching Holland? This closely?'

'No choice.'

'Where is he? Underground? Where's he going? Hang on … is that … her? The Sala soldier?'

'It is.'

'The wound of the century,' Barton said. She pulled herself up out of her chair and went as close to the autoscreen as she could without passing through it. 'No, I really don't care for it myself —'

'So you said. You always did have rotten taste.'

'— but I can recognise genius. And courage.'

'Just watch. Listen.'

Barton watched as the footage showed Holland and Sala entering the plant room. Her expression didn't change even as Sala pulled a knife, even as she ripped her clothes off and rolled in the dirt, even as they parted at street level, even as the military police moved in and arrested Holland.

'Oh, Willy. Your Willy.'

'He's not mine anymore.'

＊＊＊

Sala stood to attention before Walker in his private office. Hail sat in the corner, watching and not watching, still unsure that this was the right thing. Yes, Sala was a hero, but this idea that she could ask to see Walker — demand it, really — and that Walker would just agree, and that he'd see her immediately, seemed ludicrous. Wrong. Hail couldn't remember the last time it had happened. And yet Hail also trusted Walker — his instincts, his careful decision-making, whatever it was. Oh, sure, Hail was forever disagreeing with Walker in meetings, but that was his job: chief sounding board, head contrarian. But he worried too: how long before Walker's brain functions started failing him? Would he still be trustworthy at eighty per cent capacity? Twenty per cent? He shook away his doubts. Watch and trust, he told himself. Same as ever. But look to Curtin.

'Please sit,' Walker said to Sala, as he lowered himself gingerly into an armchair. Somewhat reluctantly, because she was more at ease standing before Walker, Sala sat too. Behind them, Hail paced.

'Thank you for agreeing to see me,' she said. 'I realise that the peace conference is such a busy time of year.

And it seems to be going on and on this year. But I have information that I didn't think could wait.'

'All right.'

'I ... I feel like a traitor even being here.'

'Don't say anything unless you want to. Feel free to turn around and leave.'

'No, I want to be here. I need to be. But I did ask for a private audience.' She glanced at Hail. 'No offence intended.'

'None taken — right, Hail?'

'Right,' Hail said. And he meant it. Observing Sala's peculiar sort of bluntness — he couldn't quite tell if it was friendly, but it was certainly honest — he was beginning to sense what he realised Walker already knew: Sala was a true leader.

'But it's not your decision to make,' Walker said to Sala. 'No offence intended, but I decide who sits in my meetings. And I tell Hail everything.'

'Eventually,' Hail confirmed. 'I'm his extra set of eyes and ears. He disregards my advice daily —'

'Hourly, sometimes,' Walker said.

'I understand,' Sala said, 'but —'

'— and he has my complete loyalty,' Hail said, 'because he sees further, he hears more, than I ever will, but he listens to me just the same. You can speak freely in front of me.'

'In any case,' Walker said, 'it's my call. Hail stays.'

'All right. I want to do the right thing.'

'Good.'

'But in the right way.'

'Good.'

'And it's big. And I'm not sure who I can trust. That's why — that's the only reason I wanted to keep things one-on-one.'

'You'll have to risk it,' Hail said.

'All right. What I need to tell you won't be easy. For you to hear, I mean. But I've never seen anything like it and —'

She paused and peered from Walker to Hail and then back to Walker. A wave of understanding passed through her.

'You already know. Don't you?'

'Every single sordid bit of it,' Walker said.

'And you're not surprised that I'm here, are you?'

'Surprised, not surprised — what difference does it make? I hoped you would find your way back to us.'

'Was last night a test?'

'Not at all,' Walker said. 'I was thoroughly surprised to find myself watching live footage of you rolling in dirt.'

'Ugh. The water got into the crevices on my face. I expect it'll kill me sometime or other.'

'If Holland said it was safe, it'll be safe. To the best of his knowledge, anyway.'

'Is he a scientist now?'

'Cleave will confirm. She's testing a sample. When she gets around to it.'

'What's going to happen to Holland?' Sala asked.

'He's in custody,' Walker said.

'Already?'

'Though that's classified information,' Hail said.

'Sala has full security clearance,' Walker said, 'as of now.'

'He's a good commanding officer,' Sala said. 'He was. A little dogmatic, but maybe that was just his age or his —'

'Hey, you're speaking to his peers here,' Hail said.

'Yes, I know, but what's true of him isn't true of everyone, I'm sure. He was stuck in his way *in the field*, in my opinion, but —'

'He's not dead. He's sitting in a room, just around the corner,' Walker said.

'— but fundamentally he was a good man. A decent man. Despite those five deaths in a month. If you don't mind me saying so, sir.

'Do you care if I mind you saying so?' Walker said.

'No. Not really.'

'Excellent,' breathed Hail.

'What was that?' Walker said.

'I was just clearing my throat, boss.'

'What do you think I should do to Commander Holland?' Walker asked Sala.

Now *this* is a test, Sala thought. She could see the shock on Hail's face — he was wondering how Walker could ask her this question — but instantly she saw Hail's expression turn to neutral. She couldn't work out his job, exactly, but she could see he was essential.

'Well?' Walker said. 'We happen not to have the luxury to meander. Much like a battle, we make decisions and we act.'

'I'm not hesitating. I'm declining to answer. I'm a sergeant.'

'Ex-sergeant.'

'Not ex by my choice. Holland is still my commanding officer so far as I'm concerned.'

'Very convenient,' Walker said.

'Did you think he was your commanding officer when you wrestled him to the ground last night?' Hail said.

'By your definition, I am now a lowly civilian. So I have no comment.'

'You had plenty to say to him last night. I've watched and listened to the whole thing,' Walker said.

'That was a private conversation. Like this one. Or are you filming me now?'

'I'll ask you again,' Walker said. 'What do you think I should do to him?'

Sala rose, stood to attention, and stared silently straight ahead. Walker glanced at Hail, who nodded imperceptibly.

'Please sit. Don't make me order you to sit … Thank you. Now, if you won't advise me what to do about

Holland, perhaps you'll tell me why not.'

'He's your friend. Your partner in revolution. You can —'

'"Revolution" is not my preferred word for what we did.'

'Fair enough. But it's my word.'

'It was more like a resuscitation.'

'Whatever. It was great, whatever word you use. We're here, aren't we? And he's your man from back then. He helped you save the world, or whatever the hell this place is. You decide what to do with him. Don't use me for cover.'

If Walker hadn't been so dizzy, he would have stood up at that moment, as a mark of respect for Sala. 'Good for you,' he said instead.

Sala gazed at Walker's face, and then dropped her eyes to his stomach. She stretched a hand out towards him. Hail jumped between them, a stun gun drawn.

Walker reached out and pushed Hail's arm aside. 'It's okay.'

'No,' Hail said. 'Boss, no.'

'Step back. She needs to see. She needs to understand. She needs to know the truth if she's going to do this.'

'If she's going to do what?' Hail said.

'If I'm going to take Holland's job,' Sala said. 'That's right, isn't it?'

'Yes. And no,' Walker said. He looked at Hail, who,

although shocked, nodded spontaneously.

Sala pulled on the zip of Walker's shirt and then yanked the shirt off him. Walker tried, but failed, to hide the pain she caused him.

'Fuck. Me,' Sala said.

She pushed the table out of the way, dropped to one knee, and rested her palm on Walker's pot belly. She made a fist and tapped his flesh. She put her damaged ear against it, listening to his innards moan. She moved her attention from sore to sore, examining, touching, sniffing. Finally, she examined his face. With one calloused finger, she rubbed one of his cheeks until she exposed a raw blister.

'So now you know,' Hail said.

'She already knew,' Walker said. 'Didn't you?'

'Everybody who sees you — on a screen, even — would know, if they only chose to look,' Sala said.

'Except,' Hail said, 'I'm pretty sure Holland doesn't know.'

Sala turned her head to the side and rubbed her damaged face all over Walker's face. When she was done, she took a step back, hope in her eyes.

'I felt nothing. Nothing at all,' Walker said. 'But I appreciate the gesture.'

'And I thought I had problems,' Sala said.

Hail barked a laugh.

***

Grainy lay in his hospital bed, starving and surrounded by starvation. The patches stuck all over his body vibrated war footage directly onto and through his skin. Autoscreens sat at all angles, crowding him, running images of battles continually. The screen in his clearest line of sight, if only he could have forced his eyes open, switched from a battle scene to vision of a little boy standing outside a closed door. Every few seconds — or was it the same image, repeated? — the boy pushed against the door, but it never opened. All of it — the battles, the boy — was futile.

Grainy let out the deepest, longest sigh. One of his bare arms fell limp by the side of the bed. He sighed again, as if mildly irritated, and died. A nurse came, accompanied by a film crew that recorded the nurse easing back the sheet and peeling the patches from Grainy's skin. The head doctor came next. She held Grainy's hand for a time.

'Leave that for now,' she said to the orderlies, who were preparing to wipe the body with cloths. 'I think this one warrants an autopsy.'

Only then, after a respectful time, after the nurse and the orderlies had backed away, giving Grainy a moment free of all help, did the war footage and the boy on the autoscreens fade away to nothing.

* * *

'Should I strip?' Sala asked. She stood in Curtin's examination room, wedged between the autopsy room and the operating theatre, on the fringe of the maze that was Walker Compound.

'There's really no need,' Curtin said. 'Cleave finally had the water tested. It won't cause you any lasting harm, though I wouldn't go washing in the stuff.'

'But did it get inside me?'

'I wouldn't worry, given the amount of Grand Lake dust you've breathed in over the years. Keep an eye on your skin.'

'Will it impact my tumours? Should I increase my treatment?'

'Look: from what I understand, you'll be needing a clear head to worry about the things that need worrying about.'

'You've heard, then?'

'Your problem, Commander Sala, is not that the water that touched you last night was dirty. Your problem is that it was clean. Well, relatively clean. Cleave says they must be treating it somehow, which means they're more organised than we thought, which means there's more of them, which means —'

'Is Walker dying? Will you take over?'

'How's that scar feeling?'

'How long has he got?'

'Does it stretch here?' Curtin prodded Sala's face and then shone a probe. 'Fascinating.'

'If that water really is safe. I mean, if you know it's safe, and you're treating Walker and God knows who else for this wasting disease, then why aren't you out standing in the rain, growing plants? What's stopping you?'

'That's the question, isn't it?' Curtin said. She turned her attention to the side of Sala's face. 'This ear: can you hear out of it?'

* * *

'Why did you do it?' Hail said to Holland. 'I can't believe you. After everything we've achieved.'

'Sorry to have disappointed you,' Holland said.

'No, you're not.'

'All right now,' Curtin said. 'I'm sure we can keep it friendly.'

Walker, Hail, and Curtin sat on one side of a table in the interview room at Walker Compound. Walker sat in the middle, sagging at times towards Curtin, at times towards Hail. Holland sat on the other side, resting his arms on the cool plastic surface.

'Do you three go everywhere together these days? Safety in numbers, eh?' Holland said.

'I'm a history buff,' Curtin said, giving Holland a wink. 'I wouldn't miss this moment for anything.'

'Why?' Hail said again. 'Come on. Give us something to work with.'

'What difference does it make?' Holland replied. 'Why are you even bothering to ask?'

'I'm trying to help you.'

'No, you're not. Anyway, I don't need your help. Don't need it, don't want it … What's going to happen to Dinn? Where is she?'

'Ah, so you do need our help?' Hail said.

'I'm just seeking information,' Holland said. 'She can look after herself.'

'Well, she's fine, since you ask for information. Her lodgings are bordering on the salubrious.'

'I'm sure.'

'She's not in any danger,' Walker said softly. 'There's no need for concern.'

'Yes, I know,' Holland replied. 'But I'd still like the details.'

'Speaking of information: who is it? Best you just tell us now, and we'll do what we can to help,' Hail said.

'Who is what?'

'Enough of these games. Who's starving?'

'He's very agitated today, isn't he?' Holland said to Walker and Curtin.

'He misses you already,' Curtin said.

'It's not your sister, she must be fit as a fiddle if she's wandering around breaking into hospitals and —'

'Her name's Dinn. And you've got no business calling that place a hospital.'

'Seen inside it, have you?' Hail said.

'What does the expression "fit as a fiddle" even mean, do you think?' Walker said.

'Something about survival of the fittest,' Curtin replied.

'Is it your mother?' Hail said.

'Are you kidding? She's the best eater in Rise. No one gets to live as long as she's lived. She loves her battle scenes, although it's true that she still talks about pepperoni pizza all the time. Drives the grandkids crazy, or so I'm reliably informed. As you'd understand, I don't get home much.' He looked at Walker. 'Do we really need this charade? Haven't I served you faithfully all this time?'

'You have.'

'And I'd do it all again tomorrow, for the right reasons. I don't see why we need to put ourselves through all this.'

'I know,' Walker said. 'I agree. But, look, indulge us. Hail needs this. Give him something so he doesn't feel so bad about losing you.'

'Hey, I'm here in the room. I can hear you,' Hail said. 'Am I the only person taking any of this seriously. What's the name of that man you were seeing? Is he the hungry one?'

'Who, Goldworth? I haven't talked to him in years. He's probably dead.' To Walker he said, 'He told me to choose between him and you. I chose you. But you know all this. Ancient history.'

'And you chose well,' Walker said.

'I don't know about that,' Curtin murmured. 'But he chose right.'

'And you can choose right again,' Hail said. 'It's not too late. Help us shut this thing down before —'

'No. You're looking to make sense of the situation from your perspective, which means you're looking at it all wrong. And you're fishing for information. I appreciate that. But I believe what I believe,' Holland said. 'Believe that, and move on.'

'That's it. That's the truth,' Curtin said to Hail. 'He's doing it because he's following his convictions, like he always has. If that doesn't make you okay about all this, nothing will. He's doing it because he's a soldier.'

'Or he was,' Hail said.

'Oh, he's more of a soldier today than he's ever been,' Walker said. 'He's just not our soldier. But he's still clever. Smart. Loyal.'

'Handsome. Virile,' Holland added.

'Brave, within limits,' Walker said.

'I just … I don't understand. I can't understand. How can you be so okay about this?' Hail said to Walker. 'And you too?' he said to Curtin.

'Would it help if you beat me up a bit?' Holland suggested. 'Throw a punch or two.'

Holland wanted to squeeze some jolliness out of Hail, so they could finish on good terms. Hail seemed to need it. But Holland was perplexed by Walker, who was seemingly so relaxed, so unfussed, and Curtin, so obviously amused. Walker had some new plan afoot — Holland could see it in his yellow eyes — and this plan, whatever it was, already involved him. Holland wasn't sure he was ready to have his dissent, his autonomy, his free will, given in service to Walker yet again.

'What do you think?' Walker said. 'Should we torture him a bit?'

'It might be fun,' Curtin said.

'No!' Hail said. 'Not unless you think it's … absolutely necessary.'

'Well, you might find it therapeutic. Nothing too awful. Maybe rip out a couple of his fingernails,' Walker said.

'Pull my earlobes,' Holland said.

'You're teasing me now. Stop it.'

'I've got a loose tooth. Why not yank it out for me?'

'I'll do it. Don't think I won't.'

'Okay, enough,' Walker said, suddenly ready for the charade to be over. 'I owe you a hell of a lot, Willy, but —'

'I wish you wouldn't call him th—'

'— but you always had lousy timing. You always were impatient. So be it, soldier.' He nodded to Hail. 'Time to sentence him.'

Hail switched into formal mode, and immediately felt more at ease. 'Stand, Commander Holland.'

Holland and Walker both stood to attention,

although Walker did so with some effort. Curtin kept her seat. Hail looked at Walker for directions. It was Hail's job to pronounce the sentence while Walker looked on impassively. But Hail had no idea what the sentence was.

'Commander Holland, this tribunal finds you guilty of treason,' Walker said, taking up the slack. 'You are stripped of your rank and dishonourably discharged, effective immediately. You will be imprisoned for the remainder of your life. Do you understand, prisoner?'

'I understand.'

Hail and Holland embraced, and then Hail fled the room. Curtin gripped Holland's shoulders, squeezed them hard. Their foreheads merged as they leant against each other.

'Be merciful to us,' Curtin whispered to him, 'when you win.'

She turned and left, and the doors closed behind her.

'You shouldn't have made Hail sit through that,' Holland said to Walker.

'He needed it. And you needed to put up with him needing it.'

Holland and Walker stood and embraced. But then Holland pulled Walker close and started scrabbling with his shirt. Armed guards stormed the room, followed by Hail. Walker, calm but exasperated, waved them out of the room.

'Let me see it,' Holland said. 'I deserve to see it.'

With a nod, Walker unzipped himself, exposing his stomach. Holland reached out but could not bring himself to touch.

'What's it like to feel nothing?'

'Curtin tells me I'm feeling something. Not much, but something. Otherwise, I'd have been dead months ago. And Hail keeps trying to find new food for me. But it's getting worse. It's only a matter of time.'

'I wish … I wish it wasn't happening.'

'Don't kid yourself that you're doing this for me.'

'Don't flatter yourself. I'm doing it for all of us. For the people. I knew there was something wrong with you. But until today, I never dreamed …'

'Well, now you can do it for the great citizenry of Shine. Barton has a job for you, if you'd like to take it. What do you say?'

'I say I like to make my own decisions.'

'Fair enough. You can choose prison. I won't make you fight for what you claim to believe in.'

Holland smiled, a little defeated, a little victorious. 'I said I like to make my own decisions,' he said. 'But I didn't say I believed I'd actually get the chance to.'

'Good.' Walker spoke into his wearable: 'Are you there, Commander? Are you close? … Good. The prisoner is ready for transportation. I'd like you to take care of it yourself. In the way we discussed.'

A moment later, Sala entered the room. Holland stood

momentarily stunned, but quickly recovered himself.

'Sergeant Sala, it's good to see you back in action.'

'It's Commander Sala,' Walker said.

'Ah, I see. I had high hopes for you. I was right.'

'Yeah, it's all about you and your fabulous judgement of people,' Sala said. 'I always worried that you were down-to-earth when you needed to dream, and that you were in a world of your own when you needed to knuckle down and get the job done. I was right.'

'Yes, you probably were.'

'Five deaths in a month. Are you proud of that? What a start! Will you be proud of five million? Fifty million? Will you grow prouder and prouder each time somebody drops dead in a muddy ditch? Will it make you stand tall?'

'She can be a touch righteous, don't you think?' Holland said to Walker.

'Damned straight,' Sala said.

'Well, you've made a grand choice,' Holland said.

'She chose herself,' Walker said.

'And I'm still here in the room,' Sala said, 'living and breathing and listening to the two of you old men chattering away like I'm a fucking ghost.'

* * *

Dinn's cell was roomy, the plastic bricks soft. And the guards were treating her well enough: politeness, armchairs, and no tough questions. They'd supplied her with cleaning cloths morning and night. Her mattress was comfortable enough. The military police — a different nondescript pair each time — had visited several times. She'd expected thugs, but all of them were bland and chatty, as if they were stopping by to make sure she wasn't too mad at them. None of them had pressed her for details of some grand plot. Perhaps, she thought, they believed that they already knew everything. And perhaps they did.

Despite their politeness — because of it — she didn't trust the military police. She'd asked them more than once what they were planning to do to her. Each time, they'd smiled in unhuman unison, as if their jaws were linked. She wondered if they were robots. She wondered, mostly, if they knew that she was Holland's sister. But she couldn't think of a safe way to ask.

As she sat pondering her options — she had none, she concluded, other than to sit and wait — an autoscreen appeared before her.

'Thank you, but I'm not hungry,' she said quietly, assuming her cell was wired.

'I encourage you to watch and learn,' an unfamiliar voice replied. Someone, she thought, who sounded important. And self-important.

'Might I ask who I am talking to?' Dinn asked.

'My name isn't important,' Hail replied, 'but I'm one

of your brother's oldest friends.'

'Oh, shit,' she muttered. 'Oh no.'

'Your secret is not known to the prison authorities. Or to your friends, though they wouldn't think any less of you,' Hail said. 'Please watch the screen. Please watch and learn.'

On the autoscreen in Dinn's cell, footage ran of twenty or so people, all with distended bellies, lying in their beds in a hospital ward. The image then moved forward in time: the same people now sat up in their beds, the glow of life evident in their skin. A couple of them were even able to stand unaided. All of the patients were eating plants: a cucumber here, an apple there. Dinn could see that the plants were props. They were too perfectly proportioned, too shiny, too healthy, like the pictures in Old Time books.

The image shifted again: a curtain behind the feeding men and women opened, revealing a mass of starving people crammed behind a pane of hard clear plastic. The starving masses screamed silently at the eaters. The film jumped from desperate face to desperate face, finally focusing on the exposed bloody teeth and gums of a woman whose face was pressed hard against the clear partition. She was stuck there, unable to break the clear wall, unable to take a step back.

Base propaganda, Dinn thought, and yet she could not fail to be moved by the starving masses. She realised, as the opening chords of 'Let's Be Tender' played, that watching the film had filled her up. Such is life, she thought, permitting herself a belch.

The screen went black, followed by the messages 'Brought to you by the City-State of Rise' and, after a moment, 'Thanks be to Walker.' Not 'Walker and Barton', Dinn noticed. Just 'Thanks be to Walker.'

As soon as the autoscreen disappeared, Dinn's cell door beeped and opened. When no guard entered, she got up and stood in the opening, peering out. The doors of the nearby cells had opened too, and her co-conspirators stood looking at each other. For a moment, none of them dared leave their cell, sensing that the guards were trying to trick them, that this was a test or the beginning of an interrogation. But then Dinn began walking, and the others fell in behind her.

They picked their way through the prison. Dinn kept finding unlocked doors and open gates that finally led them outside. They saw no one, which by now Dinn realised was not an accident. She didn't know why, but the voice, Holland's friend, had set them free.

Outside, the air had a musty odour and an opaque quality: the domefield was on. It cheered Dinn to know that it was raining above her. She longed to feel water landing on her bare arms.

A vehicle waited, the keys in the ignition. Dinn sat behind the wheel. The others piled in. They drove out the open front gate, the sentries turning their backs as Dinn turned onto a one-way road.

'Where are we going?' one of the others asked. 'Where can we go?'

'No idea,' Dinn said, speeding up. 'But we'll be okay.'

***

The first official act of hostility in the Spinach War occurred soon after Commander Sala drove ex-Commander Holland out of Walker Compound in a military jeep, escorted by an armoured vehicle. Neither Sala nor Holland spoke as they curled down the hills and onto the great flat plain of Rise. But the mood between them was convivial. Sala stayed quiet out of respect for Holland's momentous day: it wasn't every day that a hero became a traitor. She got that. Holland gazed out of his window, weighing the disappointment of his great friends — oh, how Hail had wailed when they said their goodbyes — but he also took the chance to sniff the air that surrounded Sala. She was an instant leader, his nostrils told him, unbound by old conventions, old struggles, old victories. She had his measure, unless he changed … unless he used his superior years, his long experience, to forget what he knew and start again.

They were passing through the sparsely populated fringe area of District 113 when a vehicle slammed into the armoured escort. Sala hit the brakes and reversed hard, but another vehicle emerged from a side road and forced her to stop.

'This is where you get off, I think,' Sala said. 'All right, you'd better hit me. Quick. We want this as authentic as possible.'

Holland stared straight ahead, half-lost in a tide of sadness that it had come to this: a defection, and a violent one at that. But he shook himself — time to save the world, again, he told himself. And then he elbowed Sala in the nose.

'FUCK. You're strong for an old man,' Sala said.

But when she examined herself in the rear-view mirror, there was no blood.

'Dammit. You'll have to do it again. Harder, this time. Harder.'

'It's not about "how hard". It's about taking proper aim,' Holland said.

'Thanks for the tip.'

This time, the point of Holland's elbow pushed deep into her nose, and, mercifully, blood streamed from her nostrils.

'Christ, sorry!' he said. 'I really am!'

They shook hands. They hugged, briefly. Sala wiped her bloody nose on Holland's shirt.

'Nice touch,' he said.

'See you in the warzone,' she said.

'I look forward to it.'

'Yeah, you're all aquiver.'

Sala arranged herself on the seat, lying as if Holland had knocked her out. Holland hauled himself out of the jeep and ran into a doorway, ignoring the two vehicles that had engineered his escape. One of the vehicles sped away, while the occupants of the vehicle that had collided with Sala's stood about, checking each other for cuts and bruises.

Sala sat alone with her bleeding nose. After a moment, she spoke into her wearable.

'It's done,' she said. 'He's gone. For Chrissakes, tell me that somebody got some decent footage of the carnage.'

***

'A few thousand plants: thirty or so varieties,' Barton had said when she and Walker sat together and created the future all over again. 'We need to know what the dissenters know. We need to know more than they know.'

'If we know what they know,' Walker had said, 'then we're just the same as them. We're just as bad as them. Aren't we?' He gazed at his open palm, the skin stretched thin. The webbing connecting thumb and finger began to bleed. He sighed and closed his eyes.

'Maybe so,' Barton said. 'But you agree? It's time we started a new war? A real war?'

'Our war has always been real.'

'You know what I mean: a war with new boundaries.'

'If we do this, I want no killing. Not on purpose, anyway.'

'We can write the rules. But it'll need to be a different sort of war. There will be more errors. More mess. More losers. It's inevitable.'

'And it goes against everything we've built.'

'And I say we can and should do our best. But think about it: we can't fight this war out at Grand Lake. We'll have to fight it everywhere. And it's already started. It's just that most of our citizens haven't noticed.'

'But who will police the new rules?' Walker said, shaking his head. 'Who will stop "whatever it takes"?'

'We will,' Barton said. 'You and me.'

'And what about when I'm gone?'

'Then I'll do it for both of us. And Curtin.'

She took his silence as agreement.

**

Holland jogged for an hour along an Old Time train tunnel. When he climbed back to the surface, the car Sala had promised him was waiting. The route towards Shine took him through the land he knew best: the dusty, bloodstained Grand Lake area, the scene of his triumphs, the landscape of his life. When he passed the set where

Sala had lost her face, he winced. It would have been so fitting, he thought, if she had dumped him here. He was proud of her. He knew that she would lose this new war with magnificent honour and courage.

* * *

'Oh, Willy. Your Willy,' Barton had said to Walker at the end of the meeting, before she went home to Shine to wait for everything to change.

'He's not mine anymore,' Walker had said. 'In fact, I think he might be yours. If you want him, that is.'

'Oh, but, it's hardly … You're offering him to me? You're offering me Willy?'

'Only if you want him. Maybe he's damaged goods. Maybe he's too old. Maybe he's seen too much to be useful. Maybe he just needs the quiet life. Maybe he needs a bit of prison time. He certainly deserves it. But he's yours if you want him.'

'Oh, I'll take him,' Barton said. 'But only if he's willing.'

'I haven't asked him. But he's willing.'

'He'll run my war very well, thank you very much.'

'I thought as much. But what about Commander Flint? Won't she be a bit grumpy?'

'Oh, she'll be fine. She's been telling me for over a year that she's sick of the fighting. The choreography. I've been asking her to hang on until I can find someone worthy of replacing her. She's been willing — not happy, but willing — but I can't ask her to take on our grand new plan. I'm hoping she'll agree to take charge of plant production —'

'I think it's called "growing stuff".'

'If I didn't want Holland, what would you really have done with him?'

'I would have … I … I … would have … oh no.'

Walker closed his eyes, swayed, and slumped in his chair.

'You're a terrible faker. Always have been,' Barton said.

'Yeah, it must be about time for my thirty minutes off,' Walker said. 'Curtin's orders.'

'Oh, I do believe that this is going to be a grand war,' Barton said. She looked at Walker as he pretended to shake. 'If you can hack the pace, old man.'

Walker forced a grin. He now knew the new war had to happen, but he still wasn't happy about it. He fought off a dry retch, which Barton took for more play-acting.

'I think the time is ripe to finally give our presidents something to say,' she said.

'I suppose you're right,' Walker said, his stomach heaving.

***

'People of Rise,' President Heelton said, in his best 'this time, it's serious' voice. He stood elevated on a stage, elevated too by the spring in his step. Throughout Rise, autoscreens appeared, demanding the people's attention. 'Please allow me to interrupt you this afternoon to make an important announcement.'

While he gave the city a chance to settle, his long moment of silence demonstrating the grave importance of the moment, he gazed to the back of the room, beyond the heads of the crowd assembled before him. He'd come to know that big announcements — and there was none bigger than this one — needed an audience, a breathing, heaving group of real people with real emotions and real faces.

He caught the eye of Ajok from the Department of Communications and Candour. She'd made sure he had a full room to talk to at short notice. He was glad Ajok was here, to witness history. If anyone deserved some real action — other than Heelton himself, of course — it was Ajok. She'd smiled and smiled all this time, all these years. If there was a medal for smiling, Ajok deserved it. And maybe, he thought, she would think more of him now that she had the chance to see what he was capable of. Maybe, just maybe, she would admire him as much as he admired her.

'People of Rise,' Heelton told the room and the city, 'it is my melancholy duty to inform you that last night our military guard was compelled to take Commander Holland into custody. Several hours ago, a specially convened tribunal found him guilty of treason. No trial was needed, and no legal or human rights were ignored: Commander Holland pleaded guilty.'

President Heelton allowed himself a quick glance at Ajok. What a pro she was, wearing her public smile without a hint of worry or fear.

'In consultation with Walker — thanks be to Walker — ex-Commander Holland's commission has been immediately terminated and he has been sentenced to life imprisonment. His replacement as commander is …' He paused, as an orchestral version of 'Let's Be Tender' began to play. '… the one and only Commander Sala.'

Heelton paused again while the crowd erupted, cheering and hooting and clapping at the image of Sala's face that now appeared. Ah, he thought, such loyalty, such adulation, all for getting her face shot off.

The screens switched back to Heelton's face. 'But wait, my fellow citizens of Rise, there's more. Please, stick with me now while I tell you the hardest news you'll ever hear. No, better yet, let me show it to you.'

His face disappeared, replaced with the perfectly edited version of Holland's escape: the violence of the rebel vehicles, the opportunism of Holland's elbow in Sala's face. Thirty seconds of action to signify a whole new world.

'Immediately before speaking to you all, I unilaterally closed down the annual Rise–Shine peace talks,' Heelton said. 'President Rant's permission to visit the city-state of Rise has been revoked. He is already on his way back to the city-state of Shine. Not only will there be no peace this year, but I can formally announce that we are in a new war. This is a war we can and must win. It is a very different war. It is a war that is everywhere. Keep your eyes open, my wonderful friends. Report any suspicious behaviour, but trust everyone. Barton, who we trusted, Holland, who we trusted, Rant, who we trusted, want to take away your right to watch war. To watch and to eat. They wish to attack your tenderness, your compassion. But we will prevail. Thanks be to Walker. Thanks be to the people of Rise.'

The crowd in the room with Heelton roared their approval and rushed the stage, just like Ajok had rehearsed with them. Heelton abandoned the lectern, stepping off the stage into the crowd. They lifted him up and carried him out of the room and into the street, camera crews and drones capturing the moment from every angle.

'VICTORY,' Heelton screamed. He meant his own victory, but it really didn't matter. He dropped to the ground. The cameras turned away. He looked around for Ajok, but she was inside, already going through the footage.

***

Wedge watched President Heelton's historic address from the house he had by now decided was his own. He liked living on the fringes. He'd particularly enjoyed long walks in the district, which he found as good a way as any to keep up effective surveillance. He'd chatted with the locals often enough that some of them had started chatting back. They were still wary of him, but they were friendly. And they were so much closer to normal than he'd thought possible.

On his walks, he'd started scavenging for building materials. Beggars can't be choosers, but he liked the mix of Old Time and New Time materials he was collecting. He was going to build himself a nice house within the shell of the old house. He was going to build himself a nice life too. He'd stopped sending in his daily reports. Nobody had noticed, not even Annar, whose job was to tell him what to do, and not even Bull and Boosie, who he knew got so much pleasure from laughing at his efforts. Nobody remembered him. Nobody cared. He hadn't defected. He was still drawing a salary, not that he needed it. He was available to fight in a war if anyone decided they wanted him.

* * *

Malee walked to the prison gates, which obligingly eased apart long enough for her to slip through the gap and back into the free world. She had no idea why she was being released without charge. Without comment, for that matter. Like everybody, she'd watched President Heelton's address. He'd been a little breathless, she thought. A little too eager. A little too bloodthirsty. But that was his job now, she supposed. This new war, if that's really what it was, didn't change anything for her. She had her own plans.

She could have called for a vehicle to collect her, or strolled a few blocks to a train station, but she decided to walk home. She was so stiff, she felt the need to move and keep moving. She'd stretched and walked in the exercise yard every day since they'd locked her up. And one time, when a guard noticed that she was favouring a shoulder, they'd sent her a masseuse, who had worked on her for an hour or more. But still, she had spent most of her time sitting on the floor, leaning against a wall, thinking, plotting.

It was early morning when she set out. It was dark by the time she arrived home. Walking through her home, everything seemed intact. The rooms were brighter than she'd remembered: had the authorities painted the walls in her absence or had she grown accustomed to the grey bricks of her cell?

She stepped through the back door into the courtyard. There was every likelihood, she supposed, that the military police had installed a camera or two. But she didn't care. They could watch her, arrest her again, lock her up, again and again, if they really felt the need.

She slipped a hand inside her top and felt around an armpit, in amongst the hair. When she removed her hand, it held a small packet of seeds. She'd stripped before Gaite when she arrived at the prison, but Gaite hadn't searched her, had barely glanced at her skin. Malee had kept the seeds the whole time.

She took one seed from the packet. Just one. The military police hadn't returned her boot and had offered no compensation for what she considered as the theft of a genuine Old Time antique. But no matter: she lifted a paver from the courtyard and dropped the seed into the dirt. She lifted another paver, surprised to find her stash of vials of water intact. She counted the vials. There were extras. She was sure of it.

As she dripped water onto the dirt, she half-expected the military police to come flying over the walls again. But no one came. She went inside, undressed, wiped herself clean, and fell asleep, exhausted, bemused, content. In the night, she woke, starving. She hated herself for it, but she propped herself up, cushions against the bedroom door, and watched 'The Battle of Sergeant Sala'. Such a headstrong commander she was going to make, she thought. Not that she cared one way or the other.

Several weeks later, in the dead of night, as Malee slept, a single police officer scaled the wall of her courtyard. The new seed had sprouted. A finger of green snaked up, and

Malee had tied it to a plastic stake. A single tomato, tiny and hard, sat amongst the leaves. Silently acknowledging Malee's achievement — a living plant in the middle of Rise — the police officer tipped a few grains of grey powder onto the tomato and slipped away.

In the morning, the stem was twisted and limp, and the fruit had split open and turned purple as a bruise. Malee pulled the plant out by its roots. She dropped a new seed into the ground and watered it.

'Patience. Patience,' she told herself.

***

Dinn heaved another shovel-full of dirt into the wheelbarrow. Her job, in the abandoned airport where she lived and worked, was to grow new shoots, as many of them as possible. She loved hand-watering most of all: the gentleness of it, the joy of glimpsing the first hint of green, the relationships she formed with new life before she passed the shoots over to others to turn into mature plants.

She missed her children, both of them embedded in the mainstream world of Rise, both of them still convinced that Walker's way was the right way, or at least the better of two options. But they weren't dogmatic about it, at least. They could see her point, unlike Dunk, who had signed up for Commander Sala's Home Force, and spent his nights on the roof of some tall building or other, watching for enemy incursions. He'd sent the separation documents to Holland because he didn't know how to contact her direct. She hadn't signed them. She didn't care who owned the house.

Dinn worried most about her mother, who had lived longer than she had any right to and who had too many tumours. They hadn't discussed it, not explicitly, but her mum knew what she was doing. And she certainly knew all about the crimes of Holland, her darling, forever-absent son. He wasn't merely fraternising with the enemy. He had become the enemy. Dinn supposed that she and Holland were fighting on the same side, but she found it hard to tell. He was off doing his grand thing. She supposed somebody had to be a leader, but she found all the posturing distasteful. And she doubted it helped much, in the end. But at least he had found this space just beyond the fringes of Rise, where the rain fell free.

Dinn looked out over the airport hangar. They were barely using one-tenth of the space, and they hadn't even started adapting the other empty buildings, but she believed that they had made a magnificent start. Before her stood rows and rows of plants, some of them thriving, some of them — there was no point in avoiding it — a little sickly and suspect.

Dinn was drinking a glass of water — perhaps her favourite thing to do in the world, and an act that made leaving the family behind worthwhile — when an air vehicle dropped out of the sky. (The sky. Who could believe it?)

The raid was over in seconds. The soldiers lobbed a few bombs onto the crops, shot some holes in the water tanks, injured a few rebels, scuffed up some dirt. Dinn was far enough from the action that she didn't bother to take cover. Besides, she knew that nobody wanted to be responsible for shooting the beloved sister of Commander Holland, even if he was a dirty traitor. She watched the brief battle closely, though, and was struck by the precision of the enemy soldiers. There was nothing random about the victims that they chose, or the injuries — not too major, not too minor — that they inflicted.

And to turn up in a flying machine: a helicopter, she heard one of the others call it, and she remembered. This was progress, she supposed. Or grandstanding. But if the other side — it's okay to call them the enemy, she told herself — believed the once-poison air was safe for travel, even for a short time, then she knew she was on the right side of history.

In the hours that followed, Dinn let the others survey the damage, call meetings, review security, debate on whether to move, where to move, how to move. She would keep tending to her plants: they were too small to endure disruption, and she'd already decided that she was staying put, at least until she could move the plants without losing them.

She stopped work only when her friend Moore called for her. Moore, it turned out, had a plastic bullet lodged in her thigh. In normal circumstances, the bullet would have broken down, allowing the wound to heal in a couple of weeks. But Moore's bullet sat too close to one of her tumours. The medic — a lovely young lad called Slumpe, self-trained but efficient enough, so far as Dinn could tell — had decided that the bullet must come out.

'Did you hear?' Moore said to Dinn.

Slumpe pushed a painkilling injection into Moore's leg and whispered, 'Be still, be still, be still.'

'Did I hear what?' Dinn asked.

'They say Sala herself was on the raid,' Moore said.

'I very much doubt it.'

'She's right. I saw her myself,' Slumpe said. 'Just a few seconds,' he said to Moore, 'and your whole leg should be numb.'

'Got anything for the rest of my body?' Moore asked.

'Nothing non-permanent, sorry,' he replied.

'You're a dear boy,' Moore said. To Dinn she said, 'They say the whole raid was filmed.'

'Surely not,' Dinn said.

'They say we're going to be famous.'

'Terrific.'

'Oh well. You're famous anyway. Famous by association.' Moore lifted one hand and started stroking Dinn's hair. 'Hey, Slumpe,' she said.

'Yeah, Moore?'

'I'm going to close my eyes now. Do you think you could go ahead cut that thing out of me?'

'Sure thing.'

As Slumpe took up the laser scalpel, he met Dinn's gaze. *She'll be fine*, he mouthed, and Dinn nodded. He turned an autoscreen on, watching it intently while adding a new cut to the untidy wound. Then he added a needle to the end of the laser and inserted it into the bullet. He began to gently tug.

'Let me know when you start,' Moore said, still stroking Dinn's hair.

Slumpe pulled the bullet free, dropped it in a bowl, turned the autoscreen off, and examined the wound.

'Looks good,' he murmured to Dinn. But as he reached for the tube of skin glue, the wound split wide open and hot red blood burst from Moore's leg.

'Shit, she's haemorrhaging,' Slumpe said. 'I've never seen this.'

'What do we do?'

'I don't know, push down on the wound, quick, keep the pressure on while I … Just keep pushing.'

Dinn used her whole body to push down on the wound while Slumpe prepared every tube of the skin glue he had. He lined them up.

'Okay, on the count of three, get off her,' he said to Dinn. 'Ready: one, two, three.'

Dinn rolled away and Slumpe emptied tube after tube into the wound. The flow of blood slowed and then stopped.

'Okay?' Dinn asked.

'Too soon to say,' Slumpe said. 'Oh no.'

'What?'

He pointed as the skin on Moore's thigh began to bulge. 'It's going to burst,' he said.

'What can we do?'

'With what we've got? Nothing but wait and see.'

Suddenly the noise of the helicopter filled the air. It flew low, just above the roofline, and lowered itself onto the ground beside the hangar. Sala's soldiers jumped out, arms aloft to show they held no guns. They ran through the hangar, yelling 'medical ceasefire, medical ceasefire, medical ceasefire' all the way to where Moore lay.

'I'm a doctor,' one of them said to Dinn and Slumpe. 'If you let us take her, we will save her.'

Slumpe looked at Dinn. 'I'm not sure,' he said. 'We should ask —'

'Yes. Do it,' Dinn said. 'But I'm coming too.'

The doctor nodded. Some of the soldiers lifted Moore onto a stretcher and strapped her down. They sprinted to the helicopter, dragging Dinn along behind, leaving Slumpe behind to clean up the blood, all of them — Dinn too — yelling 'medical ceasefire, medical ceasefire, medical ceasefire' as they went.

Dinn hauled herself into the helicopter. She felt it lifting off the ground, and it was like nothing she'd ever felt before. And then she turned and watched as the doctor began working on Moore's leg, only now remembering that Moore had reached out and touched her so tenderly. She wondered what it meant. Probably nothing.

***

Nights later, Geraldina and Flake and the children — the girl, now named Belt, and the boy, now named Dutch — watched footage of the raid on Dinn's plant-growing group for dinner. When the camera lingered on Sala, on her face, Geraldina and Flake roared their approval and clutched each other. The children watched them, bemused.

'Bloody treasonous bastards,' Flake murmured, as the footage scanned across the plants. 'Why don't they just line us up and kill us all?'

'Don't worry, love,' Geraldina said. 'Sala has things in hand.'

And there she was again, the last one back into the flying machine, holding her weapon above her head in victory as she lifted off the ground.

The screen went black for an instant before a plea appeared in stark white letters: 'Resist dissent'. And then, as always, came the final message: 'Thanks be to Walker.'

***

One morning, the citizens making their way through the city centre of Rise paused, as they always did, for the morning meal. As the people looked up, 'The Battle of Dry River Bed' played. It was an oldie but a goodie. But just before the key moment in the battle scene — when a soldier called Kenn loses an ear, clean as a whistle — two men disrobed right there in the middle of the street, exposing their swollen bellies, their body sores, their shrivelled genitals. The crowd shifted away. Most of them had been present for this sort of stunt before. The official advice was to politely ignore them, and to feel pity, not fury, for them. Only one or two people stole a glance at the men, who slapped their big, bold bellies and squeezed their body sores until pus oozed.

The military police arrived quickly to walk the two men away. They helped the men into a windowless van, drove them out to the Grand Lake area — the famous battlegrounds now abandoned — and left them there. The two men stood there, naked and confused, for less than a minute before a vehicle from Shine picked them up.

***

Late at night, and despite fifty or more sentries spread out around the property, a posse of dissidents broke into the secret hospital known as the National Concert Hall. Unchallenged, they reached the vast angled room, full of desperate and dying patients. They spread out, popping frozen cubes of concentrated vegetable pulp into the mouths of patients. It was a methodical exercise, well-planned and well-executed, carried out by experienced feeders. They knew which patients were critical and which could hold on until the next time.

When all of the patients had eaten — except for a woman called Patter, who refused her cube and demanded to watch 'The Battle of Burning Hair' — the military police flooded the room with light. They sauntered in, arresting three dissidents but allowing the rest to leave. A film crew took in the action, the director good-naturedly grumbling about the work required to edit out the inaction, speed the footage up, add some yelling and maybe a splash or two of blood.

As the room cleared of dissidents and police, a fleet of nurses moved in. First, they moved to the most seriously ill patients, checking their vital signs, adding notes to records, and in some cases reassuring patients that it was okay to swallow, not spit out, the strange stuff melting on their tongues.

'Who was that?' one prostrate old man asked a nurse.

'That was the enemy,' the nurse said, 'doing their bit to help you.'

A woman called Singh heard the nurse's reply. She threw back her sheet and stood up. Her legs shook, but she managed a few steps before she had to pause to rest and retch.

'What are you doing?' the nurse asked. 'It's best you stay in bed.'

'I'm going with them,' Singh said. 'You can't stop me.'

She tried to walk, managing a few more steps before she sagged at the knees.

The nurse murmured into his wearable. 'It's okay,' he said to Singh. 'They'll wait.'

Another nurse came to Singh, took her arm, and walked her out of the hospital.

* * *

The autoscreens of Rise appeared for another morning. But instead of a battle scene, Walker's face filled the screen. His real face: seared skin, sunken orange eyes. The camera then retreated to show that he was sitting at a table, a bowl of fruit and vegetables on the table. He picked up an orange, brought it to his nose, sniffed it deeply, and, after a long moment, hurled it away. With a mocking sweep of his arm, he knocked the bowl of fruit and vegetables from the table.

It took Walker a considerable effort to push his chair back. With his hands bolted to the table for support, he hauled himself up. He unzipped his shirt — his breathing harsh and uneven now, his arm bleeding from his assault on the bowl of fruit and vegetables — and exposed his distended stomach. He stared straight at the camera. He said nothing. No music backed him. He held that pose for more than a minute, long enough to be sure that the people of Rise were staring back at him, fully informed.

* * *

The robotic bird had been flying loops around Walker's bed, and fake rain falling on fake plants, for nearly thirty minutes when Curtin and Sala disabled the door's lock and forced their way into the bedroom. A film crew followed behind.

Walker lay face down on the floor. Curtin placed her open palm on his back. He did not stir.

'Is he dead?' Sala said.

'No, he's warm.' She felt his underarm. 'God, he's burning up. Help me. We need to turn him over.'

As they rolled Walker, he let out a short breath, almost a whistle, through papery lips. The manoeuvre hurt him dreadfully, but he didn't have the energy, the awareness, to complain or even to properly groan. But then, all of a sudden, he came to life. He tried to stand up, but lost his balance. Before they could catch him, he collapsed again, his torso on the bed, his legs thumping the floor. There he stayed, unmovable.

'You can leave now,' Curtin said to the camera crew.

'No, not yet,' Sala said.

'Doctor's orders. You can leave the drone camera, okay? But that's it.'

'Did you get a decent shot of him falling?' Sala asked.

'Yes,' the camera operator said. She backed out of the room, still filming, wondering if she'd just recorded the great Walker's final moments.

'Is he dead?' Sala asked again.

'He's so close to dead. We could let him go this time.'

'It's too soon.'

'Too soon for who?'

'We need him longer. Just a little longer. Do whatever you can. Whatever it takes.'

'But as a doctor —'

'It's an order.'

'I don't answer to you.'

'It's *his* order. You know it is. I'm sorry, but we have no choice. He doesn't care about death. He wants to die. But if he dies today, there will be mass starvations, famine.'

'All right. I'll do my best. But no guarantees.'

'I know.'

Curtin opened multiple autoscreens and moved them all over Walker's body, swaddling him like blankets. She stuck patches to his temples. 'Turn the Liffer Machine on,' she said into her wearable. After a moment, Walker's body began vibrating fiercely as every battle scene ever filmed rushed through him. Curtin kept the machine running as long as she dared.

227

'Stop. Off,' she said eventually. 'Off. Now. Any more than that,' she told Sala, 'and he'll burst.' She placed her flat palm on Walker's chest.

'How long until we know?' Sala asked.

'A few hours. Less, if it fails.'

As they stood over him, Walker opened his eyes, but all he saw was the plastic parrot, still circling overhead, still whistling the chorus of 'Singin' in the Rain'.

'You've got to laugh,' he murmured.

***

Cleave sat in her work room, facing fifty or more screens, all of them scrolling data or images. This was her favourite place on earth, a windowless room in which she monitored the earth. Here she read reports on water quality, soil quality, air quality, she tracked lifeforms, she typed, she interpreted data, she threw numbers together, devising strategies, abandoning them or refining them. But here she also did her hardest work, comparing everything she knew about the here and now with the state of the earth in the Old Time, before the troubles and the poisons and the climate really took hold.

Today, she had revisited a group of islands that sat in what had been called the Pacific Ocean. Once home to many thousands of people, to coconut groves, to rainforests, what wasn't submerged was covered in a murky grey sludge, out of which bent elbow trees, for the most part leafless, occasionally forcing their way up towards the dirty sky. There was a species of worm that seemed capable of eternal life, a tick that lived and died in a matter of hours, and fish that floated bloated as if dead when they were alive and then sank without trace when they actually died. But recently, inexplicably, there was something that looked something like rice poking out from a swamp. Cleave had sent a note to the section head for that region, who had sent a drone to take a sample and test it.

Notes. Messages. That's how she communicated with everyone, mostly using templates, except for Walker and Barton, who shared her counsel.

Cleave didn't mind seeing the broken world. It was what it was. Still, the need to compare, the need to look back, defeated her most days. It was hard to be productive while mourning the world. She had her method for recovery: silence, stillness, solitude. She didn't empty her head entirely. She'd tried that and found it taxing. Artificial. But she focused on one tiny element of the here and now: a single banana tree, twisted, with garish blue leaves, that appeared in a toxic desert; a species of prawn, seventy-four per cent of which were born with two tails and no head; the gradual but unmistakable decrease of toxins in the rain over the cities of Rise and Shine.

Many years ago, only a few weeks after she'd isolated

herself, she had disabled the sole door that led out of her mini-compound. She wanted no temptations to leave the work unfinished. Disabling the door still left her with two ways out of her self-imposed exile. She could climb out via the courtyard, across the roof of her compound until it met the main compound. But her ankles were wonky these days. They clicked as she walked from room to room. She doubted that she could scale a wall anymore. The other option was to break her way out. She had an Old Time sledgehammer leaning against an outside wall. A few hefty blows — her shoulders were in much better shape than her ankles — and she was sure she could break through the plastic bricks. But the sledgehammer was only for an emergency, if the isolation defeated her, or if remembering the Old Time too often got too much.

There was a third reason that would lead her to take to the wall with the sledgehammer: if she completed her work. If she were redundant. If the earth were restored to something resembling habitation.

The central autoscreen in front of Cleave showed Walker half on the bed, half on the floor. She wanted him to roll over. There would be so much more information on his face than on his scarred back. After a long moment, she moved the screen to the left. She shifted her attention to a wild thunderstorm that had just broken over the island of Barbados. She turned the volume up, and listened to the pounding rain, in real time.

ACKNOWLEDGEMENTS

I dedicate *Rise & Shine* to Zoë Gill, Thomas Berg, Millie Allington-Gill, and Laura Allington-Gill. I am lucky to live in a household full of love, tolerance, chat, big and strange ideas, and good and bad jokes. My love and gratitude to Zoë, Thomas, Millie, and Laura, and to my whole immediate and extended family. An especially big thank you to Mum, to Dad and Morag, and to Ros and John for all manner of care and support.

Martin Shaw is an attentive, enthusiastic, and accomplished literary agent. He's also a ripper human being. Many thanks, also, to Alex Adsett. Martin and Alex are two of the most committed supporters of Australian writing I have met.

For their companionship, moral support, good humour, compassion, and critical pushback, I thank these people from the bottom of my heart: Jane Rawson, Lia Weston, Jill Jones, Amy Matthews, Brian Pike, Gay Lynch, Erin Sebo, Sarah Tooth, Alice Gorman, Jo Butler, Glenn Smith, Gillian Dooley, Rebekah Clarkson, and

Celia Painter, and not forgetting friends and colleagues from the College of Humanities, Arts, and Social Sciences at Flinders University, AAWP (Australasian Association of Writing Programs), APWT (Asia Pacific Writers & Translators), and the University of Adelaide. And far too many other people to name individually.

Editors are the best, and I'm not just saying that because I am one. David Golding has ushered *Rise & Shine* into the world with care and precision. He is the most recent of a number of editors who have improved my writing and from whom I have learnt much about the art and craft of editing. Thanks to everyone at Scribe for their expertise and friendly professionalism. It's an honour to be published by the legendary Henry Rosenbloom.

A shout-out to two late, great creative artists I never got to meet, although I once saw one of them play live. When I wrote *Rise & Shine*, my soundtrack was Roky Erickson's great comeback album, *True Love Cast Out All Evil* (plus an occasional burst of Erickson's 1960s band, The 13th Floor Elevators). The cover of *Rise & Shine* features Hilma af Klint's painting *Group IX/SUW, The Swan, No. 17*, which she painted in 1915 in Sweden. Over a century later — one or two things have happened since then — and from the other side of the world, I gaze at Hilma's work and life with wonder and respect.

I wrote *Rise & Shine* on Kaurna land. The first couple of decades of the twenty-first century have been a frankly astonishing era for Aboriginal and Torres Strait Islander poetry and fiction. From Marie Munkara to Ali Cobby Eckermann, from Alexis Wright to Natalie Harkin, from Tony Birch to Ellen van Neerven, from Kim Scott to Melissa Lucashenko, and others, these writers are leading the way.

And thanks for reading.